***Something had to give and
apparently it was her.***

"Okay. Bodyguard it is." She met Sam's gaze and
felt a flush on her face that spread clear through
her. The thought of him guarding her body sent a
shiver down her spine.

"I know you're not crazy about the situation.
Neither am I. But we're stuck with each other.
The way I see it, things will go more smoothly
if you follow some ground rules."

"Let's be clear." Jamie stared up at him. "You can
list ground rules from now until hell freezes over,
but I'm not doing anything I don't want to do."

The stubbornness glittering in her eyes did
amazing things to her particular shade of hazel.
The obstinate expression canceled out the brown
and gold and turned them to bright green. And
beautiful. A man could lose ~~his~~ ~~....~~ ~~....~~ e
angry eyes.

Dear Reader,

Just as the seasons change, you may have noticed that our Silhouette Romance covers have evolved over the past year. We have tried to create cover art that uses more soft pastels, sun-drenched images and tender scenes to evoke the aspirational and romantic spirit of this line. We have also tried to make our heroines look like women you can relate to and may want to be. After all, this line is about the joys of falling in love, and we hope you can live vicariously through these heroines.

Our writers this month have done an especially fine job in conveying this message. Reader favorite Cara Colter leads the month with *That Old Feeling* (#1814) in which the heroine must overcome past hurts to help her first love raise his motherless daughter. This is the debut title in the author's emotional new trilogy, A FATHER'S WISH. Teresa Southwick concludes her BUY-A-GUY miniseries with the story of a feisty lawyer who finds herself saddled with an unwanted and wholly irresistible bodyguard, in *Something's Gotta Give* (#1815). A sister who'd do anything for her loved ones finds her own sweet reward when she switches places with her sibling, in *Sister Swap* (#1816)— a compelling new romance by Lilian Darcy. Finally, in *Made-To-Order Wife* (#1817) by Judith McWilliams, a billionaire hires an etiquette expert to help him land the perfect society wife, and he soon starts rethinking his marriage plans.

Be sure to return next month when Cara Colter continues her trilogy and Judy Christenberry returns to the line.

Happy reading!

Ann Leslie Tuttle
Associate Senior Editor

Please address questions and book requests to:
Silhouette Reader Service
U.S.: 3010 Walden Ave., P.O. Box 1325, Buffalo, NY 14269
Canadian: P.O. Box 609, Fort Erie, Ont. L2A 5X3

TERESA SOUTHWICK

Something's Gotta Give

Buy
-A-
Guy

SILHOUETTE *Romance*®
Published by Silhouette Books
America's Publisher of Contemporary Romance

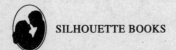 SILHOUETTE BOOKS

ISBN 0-373-19815-9

SOMETHING'S GOTTA GIVE

Copyright © 2006 by Teresa Ann Southwick

This edition published by arrangement with Harlequin Books S.A.

® and TM are trademarks of Harlequin Books S.A., used under license. Trademarks indicated with ® are registered in the United States Patent and Trademark Office, the Canadian Trade Marks Office and in other countries.

Visit Silhouette Books at www.eHarlequin.com

Printed in U.S.A.

Books by Teresa Southwick

Silhouette Romance

Wedding Rings and Baby Things #1209
The Bachelor's Baby #1233
*A Vow, a Ring, a Baby Swing #1349
The Way to a Cowboy's Heart #1383
*And Then He Kissed Me #1405
*With a Little T.L.C. #1421
The Acquired Bride #1474
*Secret Ingredient: Love #1495
*The Last Marchetti Bachelor #1513
**Crazy for Lovin' You #1529
**This Kiss #1541
**If You Don't Know by Now #1560
**What If We Fall in Love? #1572
Sky Full of Promise #1624
†To Catch a Sheik #1674
†To Kiss a Sheik #1686
†To Wed a Sheik #1696
††Baby, Oh Baby #1704
††Flirting with the Boss #1708
††An Heiress on His Doorstep #1712
§That Touch of Pink #1799
§In Good Company #1807
§Something's Gotta Give #1815

Silhouette Special Edition

The Summer House #1510
  "Courting Cassandra"
*Midnight, Moonlight &
  Miracles* #1517
It Takes Three #1631
*The Beauty Queen's
  Makeover* #1699

Silhouette Books

*The Fortunes of Texas:
  Shotgun Vows*

*The Marchetti Family
**Destiny, Texas
†Desert Brides
††If Wishes Were…
§Buy-A-Guy

TERESA SOUTHWICK

lives with her husband in Las Vegas, the city that reinvents itself every day. An avid fan of romance novels, she is delighted to be living out her dream of writing for Silhouette Books.

Do you need a man?
The 75TH semi-annual
Charity City Auction

This is your chance to find the right one
for that "honey do" list.

Could you use a weekend warrior? Ex-Army Ranger
Riley Dixon is the guy for you. He's donating a survival
weekend guaranteed to get your heart rate up.

What about that home repair you've been putting off?
Dashing Des O'Donnell, former Charity City High
football hero, now owner and president of his own
construction company, is offering a repair of your choice.

Personal security issues? Defend your honor?
Savvy Sam Brimstone, recently of the LAPD
and a hotshot detective, is your man.

These are just a sampling of the jaw-dropping guys
available to the highest bidder. Ladies, don't miss the
chance to buy a guy—no strings attached.

Cash, check, credit and debit cards gratefully accepted by
the Charity City Philanthropic Foundation.

Chapter One

If anyone had told him he'd wind up on the wrong side of the law, Sam Brimstone would've said they'd taken one too many shots to the head.

But here he was looking up at the beefy, balding judge who stared right back at him from the bench. "Samuel Owen Brimstone, the charge against you is one count of assault and battery. How do you plead?"

There was the sixty-four-million-dollar question. Once upon a time Sam had been a decorated detective with a big-city police department, working for law and order. Now the law in Charity City, Texas had its sights locked and loaded on him. That's what he got for butting into something that was none of his business. He'd be back on the highway doing seventy-five miles an hour to nowhere if he hadn't decked a bozo hustling a hard-working bar-and-grill waitress.

Where the gray area came in was that Sam knew he'd been spoiling for a fight, and the bozo had obliged by giving him motive and opportunity.

"Mr. Brimstone, the court doesn't have all day. Did you, or did you not, start an altercation last night at the Lone Star Bar and Grill?"

"Depends on your definition of altercation."

"Can I take that as a yes?"

"Yes, what?" Sam asked.

"Yes you threw the first punch."

"You can."

"Can what?" the judge asked, barely controlling his exasperation.

Sam smiled. Small consolation that his initials spelled SOB and he was living up to them. A man had to take comfort wherever he could. "I threw the first punch, Your Honor."

"Do you have anything to say for yourself?"

"He had it coming."

"Anything else?"

"No."

"So you're pleading guilty?"

Sam was guilty of more than assault and battery. It was the reason he'd left the LAPD. A woman had died because of him. The law didn't hold him accountable, but his conscience was something else. So he'd take re-sponsibility for hitting a guy who deserved it. Besides, he didn't have any priors. Probably he'd get off with a warning and a lecture about anger management, then be on his way.

"Yes." He noted the judge's raised eyebrow and decided not to push it. "I'm pleading guilty."

"Okay, son. I'm sentencing you to thirty days community service."

"Thirty days!" What the hell was going on? He'd already spent the night in jail for doing the wrong thing, right reason. "That seems excessive," he said, suddenly developing an anger-management problem. "I'm just passing through town. Anywhere else, these charges would be dismissed with time served."

"This isn't anywhere else. It's Charity City." He glared down from the bench. "Do you have somewhere else you need to be?"

"No, sir. I'm between jobs."

"Is there a financial hardship putting yourself up in town? If so, the county would be happy to arrange accommodations," the judge said pointedly.

"Thanks, anyway, but I've sampled cell block hospitality. I can afford a room."

He was pretty well off, thanks to all work, no play, a side job doing private investigations and the hefty inheritance his bastard of a defense attorney father had left him, even though he didn't want any part of dear old absentee Dad's blood money. But the judge didn't need to know any of that.

"Okay, son, it's the opinion of this court that thirty days is a fair and equitable sentence."

"I've seen armed robbers get less than thirty days," Sam blurted out angrily.

"Keep talking and I can go forty-five." Sam started to protest, and the judge's eyes narrowed in warning. He closed his mouth and Judge Gibson continued. "Your thirty days will be auctioned off at the philanthropic public sale that we here in Charity City like to call Buy-a-Guy. Proceeds go to a foundation to fund the town's charitable endeavors."

"Let me get this straight," Sam said. "I'm being sold for thirty days?"

"That's about the size of it."

"Last time I checked, buying and selling human beings was against the law."

"It still is. This is community service."

"What do I have to do?"

"Your pertinent information will be listed on the town Web site and anyone who's in need of your particular skills will pay for them."

"What if I don't have any skills?"

The judge looked down at the paperwork in front of him. "Says here you're LAPD. A detective. Retired. You any good?"

"At being retired?" Sam shrugged. There was that whole SOB thing again. "Haven't been at it long enough to find out."

"Smart-ass you're good at," the judge commented wryly. "What about police work?"

"I put away my share of bad guys." Some he couldn't keep behind bars.

"I know someone who could use a good detective."

"So this is a setup." Sam wasn't asking. The crafty old judge had known his background and availability when he'd handed down the sentence.

"No. You broke the law. These are the consequences."

"Harsh consequences given the circumstances."

"Guess you shouldn't have given up your right to an attorney. And remaining silent wouldn't have done you any harm, either."

This wasn't the first time he should have kept his mouth shut. "I want to change my plea."

"Can't. It's already entered into the record."

Sam was seething. "I'm being scammed and we both know it."

"You say scam, I say justice. Since I'm the one wearing the black robe, my say goes." The judge glared as he pointed. "And before you open your mouth again, I'm warning you. One more outburst and you've got sixty days."

Sam clenched his jaw.

The irony was he hadn't intended to stop in this town, but the highway billboard had caught his attention. Charity City, The Town That Lives Up To Its Name. Then he'd remembered that his friend Hayden Blackthorn had moved here to open a branch office for his company, Blackthorn Investigations.

That's when Sam had decided to pull into the Lone Star Bar and Grill in order to look up his old friend. Charity might begin at home but he was a long way from there.

"I think your parents bought you a man last night."

"No way, Abby."

"Yes, way."

Jamie Gibson had thought that eating lunch in her office would be less stressful than hassling a crowded restaurant. Now she wasn't so sure. Abby Walsh had become her friend after she'd handled her divorce from a husband as flaky as a French pastry. The guy had gone to Hollywood to audition for a reality show and never came back. More proof, as if Jamie needed any, that men couldn't be counted on.

"My parents bought a man?" She shifted the phone to her other ear as she unwrapped her sandwich. That revelation cranked up her stress level by a couple notches.

"Yeah. You weren't at the auction last night to keep them in line," Abby said.

"I had briefs to write."

"Riddle me this—if you have to work overtime to write them, why are they called briefs?"

"Named by a man," they both said together.

"I'd much rather have spent the evening with you and Molly," Jamie added, taking a sip from her drink.

Her gaze slid to the framed picture on her desk of herself with her two friends—brown-haired, blue-eyed Abby Walsh and redheaded Molly Preston. She'd hated missing her evening with them. And apparently it wouldn't have hurt to keep an eye on her folks. "What happened? They bought a man?"

"First things first. I got the ex-army ranger."

Jamie frowned. "The one who donated the weekend campout you wanted?" She was dying to take a bite of her sandwich but didn't want to chew in her friend's ear.

"That's the one. Kimmie is determined to get her Bluebonnets outdoor badges, and since I don't know a tent pole from a fishing rod, Riley Dixon is our man. He donated the weekend for sale because the foundation gave him the start-up capital for his security business."

"Good for him." Jamie knew that Abby's daughter would be thrilled with the campout. "Now what about my folks?" she prompted.

"Yeah. I'm getting to that. But first I have to tell you about Molly."

"Okay. But can you move it along. You're killing me here, and I've got to eat my lunch. This is like waiting for the other shoe to fall."

"If you'll stop interrupting, I'll tell you everything." She took a breath. "Molly made me bid on Des O'Donnell."

"Didn't Des take over the family construction company after his father passed away?"

"Yes. And he donated a home repair for auction

because his company got the contract to do the new wing at the preschool where Molly teaches."

"And she made you do the bidding?" Jamie asked.

"Yeah. I have no idea why she was being so secretive, but everyone thinks I bought *two* men. Mayor Wentworth had some fun with that."

"I bet he did. So are you finished toying with me yet? What did my parents do?"

"One of the guys for sale was an ex-LAPD detective and they bought him."

Jamie groaned, suddenly losing all interest in her food. "Probably not for a busboy at the restaurant."

"I don't think so. Your folks give new meaning to the words overprotective," Abby agreed. "I'm sure they'd have followed you and Stu to New York if they could have found a way."

Anger and pain sliced through Jamie along with memories of that time. Stu had urged her to go with him to the big city, and, starry-eyed and in love, she'd agreed. Her parents had been deeply disappointed that she'd be so far away, not to mention disapproving of the guy she'd be so far away with. They'd been right, as it turned out. Shortly after the move, Stu had walked out on her.

"I almost wish they had come with us," Jamie said. "But I'm sure the phone company is grateful they stayed in Charity City and racked up a gazillion long-distance minutes."

She worked at making light of it, but the pain of that time—not just Stu's abandonment, but what happened after—she'd never get over it. And she couldn't talk about it with the people who mattered most. All anyone knew was that he'd broken it off. Her parents worried about her too much, and she'd learned to keep things from them—ironically, to protect them. She'd never tell them what she'd gone through alone.

And now it was in the past. What doesn't kill you makes you stronger, and the loss she'd suffered had made her strong enough to face almost anything.

"Yeah," Abby said. "Stu was a jerk."

If you only knew how much, Jamie thought. "He probably still is. But I do wish my parents would learn to let go."

"So, I guess you didn't know about their Buy-a-Guy purchase?"

"You guess right." She sighed and wrapped up the untouched sandwich. "When I got back to the office after court this morning, there was a message from my mom. That's probably why she called."

"There's always a chance it has nothing to do with you."

Jamie laughed. "Very funny. There's a better chance that I could flap my arms and fly to the moon."

"Yeah. Well. At least forewarned is forearmed."

"Always looking for the silver lining, huh, Ab?"

"What can I say? I'm a glass-is-half-full kind of gal."

"Thanks for the heads-up. Give Kimmie a kiss for me."

"Will do. Take care. Good luck. Bye."

After hanging up, Jamie looked at the message slip

again. Forewarned *is* forearmed, she thought. She couldn't return the call now because their restaurant was always busy at lunchtime, and besides, it was time for her to get back to work. But they would definitely talk after the dinner rush, and Jamie would make a case for discouraging the folks from whatever interfering they had planned.

"You always work this late?" The voice was gravel rough and breathtakingly masculine.

Heart pounding, Jamie swiveled her chair away from her computer monitor and faced the man in the doorway. She hadn't been expecting anyone and the interruption startled her. He was big, probably just over six feet. His brown hair was cut short, and his eyes were the most unusual pale shade of blue. The black T-shirt he wore tucked into worn jeans was molded to an impressive set of muscles on his upper chest and arms. And he was magazine-cover handsome. Stu had been handsome, too. Probably still was, she thought irritably.

"Office hours are over," she said. "I can see if there's an appointment available tomorrow…"

One very broad shoulder lifted lazily. "That's not why I'm here."

He stirred then, every movement graceful and sort of predatory as he strolled closer. Jamie stood, for all the good it would do her. If he meant her harm, the best she could do with her own five foot two, 105 pounds, would be to put up token resistance. Make too big a mess to cover up. Scratch him. Get DNA under her fingernails. And . . .and nothing. She'd been watching too much *Law and Order* on TV, she realized.

He kept moving until he got to her desk. "Name's Sam Brimstone. So what's a nice girl like you doing in a place like this?"

Hmm. "You don't approve of law offices?"

"It's not the building. It's the ethics."

"You don't like lawyers."

"Chalk one up for the counselor."

"If you feel that way, why are you here?" Her gaze narrowed. "Did my parents send you?"

"Yes. I guess you might say I'm your bodyguard."

Oh, great. So much for intercepting her mother and talking her out of the plan. But one could never go wrong being polite.

She held out her hand. "Jamie Gibson. Nice to meet you."

"Same here." His large palm all but swallowed hers. "By the way—nice people your folks."

"Yes, they are. But I don't get it," she said, then let out a long breath. "My parents are so overprotective they'd wrap me in plastic and put me on the shelf if they could. And you're a total stranger. Why would they trust you?"

It was one thing to buy the time a man donated for auction, but making him her bodyguard was something else.

"They checked out my references."

"And those are?"

"While I was with the LAPD, I moonlighted and did some work for Hayden Blackthorn."

"Of Blackthorn Investigations?"

"You know him?"

She nodded. "This law office has used the agency's services, and my parents have become good friends with him and his mother, Margaret, since they moved to Charity City a couple years ago."

"Hayden and I knew each other pretty well. Apparently, he said some good stuff because Roy and Louise acted like I have wings and a halo."

He was on a first-name basis with her parents? "So, is that why you moved here? To work for your friend?"

"Nope. I just dropped in to say hi."

"Then I don't get it. Why would you volunteer time for the auction?"

"Wasn't exactly voluntary. More in the nature of community service. Judge Gibson—"

"Uncle Harry?"

His eyes narrowed, and he crossed his arms over his wide chest. "I thought something was fishy."

"What do you mean?"

"For starters, the punishment should fit the crime. I stopped in the bar for a beer. While trying to mind my own business, Bo Taggart decided to play fast and loose with one of the waitresses and I decked him."

"In my humble opinion, Mr. Brimstone, you've

already done the community a service. Why would my uncle be so tough?"

"Because I played into his hands by pleading guilty."

Oh, great. A family conspiracy. "Surely your attorney advised against it," she protested.

"Didn't have one. Like I said, I don't believe in them."

Hmm. A cop who didn't believe in attorneys. He probably had his reasons, but she didn't want to know. The sooner they settled this misunderstanding, the better.

"And so here you are doing community service for…"

"Thirty days."

Her eyes widened. "You must have really ticked him off."

"And vice versa. When I called him, on the scam in progress, he threatened me with sixty days to deal with my anger-management issues."

She couldn't say that she wouldn't feel the same under the circumstances. But maybe there was more Sam wasn't saying. "My uncle is a good, fair judge. Why would he throw the book at you?"

"Because he could."

"Define *could*."

"I'm between jobs and it's not a financial hardship to put myself up here in town for thirty days. And—"

"There's more?"

"Oh, yeah. I used to be a detective. The town auction was coming up. And your family thinks you need a cop on your side."

Jamie recalled Abby telling her about his police

background. "Are you any good?" As soon as the words were out of her mouth, the double meaning hit her and a blush crept into her cheeks. "What I mean is—"

"I get your drift." One corner of his mouth curved up before his frown returned. "Uncle Harry asked the same question. Some people thought I was a good detective, but they were wrong."

"Why is that?" she asked, looking into blue eyes that had probably seen too much. No, no, no. Curse her soft-hearted streak. She refused to get sucked in, and held up her hand. "Forget it. I don't need to know."

What she needed was to get back to work. And to do that, she had to get Sam Brimstone out of her office. Buying her a man had crossed the line. Even by her parents' standards.

"Look, Mr. Brimstone—"

"Sam."

"Okay. Sam," she repeated, annoyed at the husky tone that slid into her voice. "Here's the thing, my parents arranged all this without my knowledge. They promised—"

"What?"

"It doesn't matter." She could see the questions in his eyes and wasn't going there. "The point is if I'd known what they had in mind, I'd have stopped them."

"They've got their reasons. Why don't you tell me what's going on," he suggested.

She could at least do that. He would see why the bodyguard thing was over the top.

"I've had a series of hang-up phone calls in the middle of the night."

"Heavy breathing?" he asked.

"No."

Not until now. With him. A man who was the walking, talking definition of raw sexuality. And how inappropriate was she? This wasn't a half hour episode of *Sex and the City*. This was real life. Her life. And she didn't want a guy complicating things. Especially a stranger who was just passing through.

A man she'd known in law school and moved across the country to be with had dumped her and turned his back when she was losing their baby. The miscarriage was the worst thing she'd ever been through. If there was any up side—and that was a big *if*—she'd learned a valuable lesson. When the going gets tough, men just keep on going, and she didn't care to count on another one. On top of that, her family had apparently conspired against Sam. Why would he be sympathetically disposed toward her?

"Did he ever say anything?" Sam prompted.

"Hmm?" She blinked and tried to focus her thoughts. "Oh. No. He just calls between midnight and four in the morning. It was every night for a while."

"You could have turned it off."

"I finally did." When exhaustion had set in. Unfortunately fatigue had loosened her tongue and she'd mentioned to her folks what was going on. "I still had my cell for emergencies, but then he started calling that number."

"Your father said a photo of you is missing from his desk at the restaurant."

She nodded. "Someone left the frame and just took the picture."

"I see." He rested a hip against the corner of her desk. "Did you report this to the police?"

"Yes. And they investigated. Followed every possible lead and came to a dead end. There wasn't much to go on." She sat in her chair, putting a little distance between them.

"I see," he said again.

"Then the calls just abruptly stopped. I haven't had one for several weeks now. My theory is that it was someone who was venting about something and the police involvement brought them to their senses. And now they're over whatever was bugging them."

"And your point is?"

She folded her hands on her desk. "I'm not an idiot. If I was the heroine in a bad B movie, I wouldn't go outside to face the serial slasher without a well-equipped army. The police would be actively involved if there were a concrete threat. And let's be clear, this harassment wasn't even very original."

"As harassment goes you'd prefer a horse's head under your pillow?" he asked wryly.

"Very funny. You know what I mean. I'm no hero. If there was reason to be concerned, I'd have picked out my own bodyguard."

One who looked nothing like Sam. A shorter guy with zero sex appeal and absolutely no animal magnetism.

"You're a family law attorney, right?" he asked, lasering her with his blue-eyed gaze as he leaned forward and flattened his palms on her desk.

"Yes. Says so on the sign out front."

"Then I'm sure you're aware that domestic disturbance is the most volatile and deadly situation a cop faces."

"Yes, but—"

"But, nothing. When families are involved, emotions run high."

"And your point is?"

"Never underestimate anyone or anything. Ever."

She stood, but still had to look up at him. "Good advice, Sam. I'll keep it in mind. Thanks for stopping by. I sincerely apologize for any inconvenience my family caused you."

His gaze narrowed. "You're throwing me out?"

"Not literally."

She couldn't manage to stop herself from assessing the muscles straining the sleeves of his T-shirt. If they were arm wrestling, he'd take her easily. But this was her office, her turf—and she called the shots. She was giving him leave to leave.

It was a preemptive strike. He was good-looking enough to make her knees weak and had enough character to get between Bo Taggart and the woman he was attempting to grope. There could be a lot to like about this man, and thirty days joined at the hip could do her a lot of emotional damage. Assuming he stuck around that long.

She wasn't willing to chance it.

She put her hand out. "Goodbye, Sam."

His eyes narrowed dangerously. "Not so fast, Counselor."

Chapter Two

"Excuse me?" Jamie's eyes grew wide with surprise. "'Not so fast'? This is my office and I can do things at any speed I choose. And I choose for you to hit the road. Don't let the door hit you in the fanny on the way out."

"I'd like nothing better than to shake your hand, say, It's been nice but I've got places to go and people to see, you should have a good life."

"But?"

"But I can't. And there are two very good reasons." Sam watched her gaze narrow.

"Such as?"

"Number one—no matter how unfair it is, I'm under a court-mandated sentence to perform community service."

"And number two?" she asked.

"Your parents believe there's a threat to your safety."

"My parents believe I'm at risk unless I'm with them or at home with padlocks on the doors and windows."

Funny, he thought. Her parents had told him she'd be stubborn. And she was. But they'd neglected to mention that she was beautiful. And she *definitely* was.

Brunette curls brushed her shoulders and framed her oval face dominated by big hazel eyes with thick, dark lashes. She wasn't very tall, maybe five-one or -two and slender, which tapped into the protective streak he tried to ignore. He'd protect her, but it wouldn't get personal. And he didn't even want to get started on the slight indentation in her chin that might be a shadow but begged for a more-thorough investigation. Exploration of that particular area, or any area for that matter, wasn't going to happen.

He stared down at her. "If I learned anything as a cop, it's not to take any threat too lightly." The lesson had been costly. His best friend's sister had paid with her life. If he made the mistake again, what happened to her would all have been a waste, and he could never find a way to live with that.

"Look, Sam, you're right about my parents. They're lovely, caring people. But if you're their daughter, those qualities are a double-edged sword."

"Oh?"

Here it comes, he thought. Lawyer spin. He folded his arms over his chest and rested a hip against her desk, settling in for the long haul. At least the view was good, he thought, letting his gaze trace the defined curves and fullness of her mouth.

She cleared her throat. "When I was a kid, I practically had to get a dispensation from the pope to go out on a date, and even then, until I was over eighteen, my father either came along or shadowed us in his car."

"You don't say."

"Then I insisted on going away to college, thinking I'd leave and find some independence."

"And you didn't?"

"A little. But they rented an apartment near campus and one or both of them were there a lot of the time. If they didn't have a restaurant to run, they'd probably have gone to class with me." She sighed. "I adore my mother and father, but their meddling reached the saturation point. And I'm sure they'd have followed me to New York if they could have found a way."

"New York?" He noticed something about her. A subtle change.

"After law school, I went to work for a firm in New York." She shrugged. "It looks good on a résumé."

Uh-huh. As a detective, he'd done more interviews than the Human Resources Department at a Fortune 500 company. He'd found body language as revealing as dialogue. And when Jamie mentioned moving to the Big Apple, a look in her eyes, tightening around her mouth, told him there was more to it than beefing up her work history. It was personal. And he wanted to know about the guy, but he let it go. For now.

Besides, she was preaching to the choir on this over-protective thing. As far as the Gibson family looking out for her, he was an innocent bystander who'd got sucked in. Well, maybe not lily-white innocent, but almost. He didn't even care that the money paid for his community service was going for a good cause. He intended to do his time and get the hell out of town. No harm, no foul.

"Are you finished?" he asked. "With lawyers, some-times it's kind of hard to tell."

"I could be."

"How will I know?"

She picked up a pen and tapped it on the pile of papers in front of her. "Are you convinced my folks are overreacting and that I have no need for a bodyguard?"

"I'm convinced that your family went to considera-ble trouble and expense to make sure nothing happens to you for the next thirty days."

"Okay, so you get it—"

He held up his hand and straightened to his full height. "I also know for a fact that I assured Roy and Louise that on my watch, I will do everything humanly possible to find out who's harassing you."

She stared at him for several moments. "Was I talking to myself? We don't know there is anyone harassing me. So any investigation would be a waste of time."

"But it's the court's time, purchased by your parents."

"Without my knowledge or consent."

She stood and stared him down—eye to eye. Well,

not technically. He towered over her, but the glare she was giving him canceled out any height advantage.

"So, what we have here is a standoff," she said.

"Stalemate. Deadlock, draw, impasse," he agreed. "I'd say something's gotta give."

"I'm not going to blink."

"Me, neither."

She put her hands on her hips. "When this happens in court, we go to mediation."

"I'm not going in front of Uncle Harry again, if that's what you're getting at."

Her mouth twitched as she fought a smile. "I was thinking we should go in front of my folks at the restaurant."

"And do what?" he asked suspiciously.

"Get them to give you absolution. Release you from this obligation."

It would be a waste of time. Jamie got her stubborn gene from one or both of them. He knew that because he'd tried to tell Roy and Louise he wasn't the right man for this job. They refused to believe him after Hayden Blackthorn's glowing reference. But he was getting nowhere here. So…

"Okay," he said.

"Okay," she agreed.

He waited for her to gather up her jacket, purse and briefcase before they left and locked her door. At the end of the hall a man stood in an office doorway.

"Jamie, are you leaving?"

"Hi, Al. Yeah. Something's come up."

Al considered Sam. "Is he a friend of yours?"

"Sam Brimstone," Sam said, holding out his hand.

"Al Moore."

The guy had up-and-comer written all over him. Young, good-looking, a firm aggressive handshake. And Sam didn't like him.

"Al's an attorney here at the firm," Jamie explained.

"I thought we were firm friends, too."

"Of course," she said, shaking her head at his pun. "You're always there for me."

"Good to know." He looked at Sam. "People make the job, and friendships are what make the long hours tolerable."

"Isn't that the truth?" she agreed.

Al grinned, the effects of his white strips so bright, Sam was tempted to whip out his shades. And again he picked up a whole lot of unspoken communication from body language and what Slick *didn't* say. This guy wanted Jamie, and there was nothing friendly about it. Lust—pure and simple. It glowed in his eyes, and the tension was there in every muscle in his twenty-four-hour-fitness toned body.

Sam *really* didn't like this guy.

It wasn't jealousy, he told himself. He barely knew Jamie, certainly not well enough to be jealous of her co-worker. And he didn't want to know her better because a detective should never get personal with a person involved in a case.

She looked at the watch on her wrist. "Well, we have to be going."

Al slid his hands into the pockets of his tailored slacks. "So where are the two of you headed?"

"Dinner," Sam said, putting his palm at the small of her back, the gesture intimate, but only to urge her forward.

The guy's smile disappeared faster than you could say "teeth bleach," and Sam felt a surge of satisfaction that told him he really had to work on that SOB thing. And he would. Real soon, he thought, escorting Jamie to the elevator.

Jamie drove to the restaurant with Sam on her tail in his sleek, black Mustang. They went into The Homestead through a back entrance, and she knew Sam was following her, this time on foot. Even if she hadn't heard the heavy sound of his boots behind her, she could just *feel* him. His presence raised the hair on the back of her neck and tingles everywhere else. Back in her office, she'd sworn he was staring at her mouth. But she was probably wrong. He'd stopped in town to say hello to a friend, and her family had turned his life upside down. Why in the world would he be thinking about kissing her?

She turned a corner and poked her head into the room her folks used as an office. As usual, paperwork was scattered around the computer on each of the two desks facing each other from opposite walls. Two desks, two computers, and neither of her parents was anywhere in sight.

"They must be out front working," she said.

"Do they always leave the back door unlocked?"

His body was so close behind her she could almost feel his chest against her back and the vibrations of his deep voice. There was no mistaking the disapproval in his tone.

"I don't know," she admitted.

"Anyone could have walked in and helped themselves to anything in here, including the picture of you that your parents told me was stolen."

"Even if it was locked, this place is so busy at lunch and dinnertime that it would be easy to slip back here unnoticed."

"I need to have a talk with them about security."

Before she could respond, there were footsteps in the hall. Sam moved farther into the room and stood beside her, just before her parents appeared in the doorway.

"Jamie." Her mother held out her arms, and Jamie went into them.

"Hi, Mom." She gave her father a quick, hard hug. "Dad. You already know Sam."

"Louise. Roy," he said.

They shook hands, Sam towering over the other man, Jamie noticed. Roy and Louise Gibson were like a matched set, one complementing the other—both small and round and solid and comfortable. Her mother's short brown hair was shot with red highlights to cover the gray. What hair her father had left encircling his head was gray. He always said he'd earned every single one worrying about his only daughter. They were both dressed for the evening crowd—her father in a navy suit and red tie, her mother in a long-sleeved black knit dress and matching low-heeled shoes.

"I see you and Sam have met," her father said.

Jamie huffed out a breath, then leaned against her mother's littered desk, folding her arms over her chest.

Before she could say anything, her mother asked, "So, why are you upset?"

"Let me count the ways," she mumbled.

"What?" Her mother's expression grew wary.

Jamie shot Sam a look that said this was all his fault, then cocked a thumb in his direction. "You guys have some explaining to do."

Her mother sighed. "We have a nice quiet table in a cozy corner. How about we sit down, have something to eat. Maybe a nice glass of wine. We can talk."

"I don't want food. I don't want wine. I want some answers." She glanced at them both. "So?"

Louise shrugged, clearly unapologetic. "So, we bought him at the auction."

"What were you thinking?" Jamie asked.

Roy moved beside her and put his arm around her shoulders. "He's a detective from Los Angeles."

"Used to be," Sam clarified.

In the doorway, he casually rested a shoulder against the door frame, as if he was holding it up. As wide as his shoulders were, he almost could. A man in the prime of his life, yet he'd left LAPD. Why? Jamie wondered.

"Whatever," her father said. "L.A.'s loss is our gain. For thirty days we don't have to worry about our little girl."

Jamie struggled to keep the irritation from her voice. "You don't have to worry about me at all. And I'm not a little girl."

She made the mistake of looking at Sam as she said that. Something sparked in his eyes, a very male response that confirmed he agreed she was all grown-up. It was almost enough to distract her, but not quite.

"You'll always be little to us," her mother was saying. "We're your parents. We changed your diapers—"

"Okay." Jamie held up a hand. On the upside, at least all the naked baby pictures were at their house. "No one's arguing about the family connection. But you guys have got to stop treating me like a china doll."

"We're just concerned. Maybe he can figure out who's harassing you and make them stop," Roy said. "He finds perps. It's what he does."

"Used to," Sam said again.

"Dad, you've been watching too many cop shows on TV." Jamie sighed. Maybe she should approach this from a different direction. "So why didn't you guys tell me what you'd done?"

The folks exchanged a guilty look. "Didn't your receptionist tell you I called?" her mother asked.

"Yes. But—"

"You could have called back."

"You could have tried my cell. Since when do you go through the switchboard?"

"I think maybe cell phone reception isn't so good in your office."

"Since when?" Jamie demanded.

"I tried," her mother said. "Apparently you were busy today."

"I'm busy every day and I always get your calls. You guys aren't very good fibbers. You're so busted."

"Okay." Louise met her gaze. "We went ahead and bid on him at the auction, but we knew you'd say no."

"And just turned him loose on me without warning?" she scolded, then met Sam's gaze. He'd been a victim in all this, too. Although the humor glittering in his eyes didn't make him look very victimlike.

"We didn't want to hear how you don't need anything and can take care of yourself." Louise looked at Sam. "She's our miracle child. We tried for years and couldn't get pregnant—"

"Mom—"

"He should know how we feel," she defended. "Just when we gave up trying—to have a baby," she clarified. "We didn't give up sex."

"Too much information, Mom."

Just shoot me now, Jamie thought, her cheeks warm with humiliation. Then she made the mistake of looking at Sam again. Amusement cranked up several notches in his eyes. At least someone was having a good time here.

"That's when it happened," her mother continued. "We were pregnant. Then she was born. Our little girl. Our very own miracle."

"Look, guys, I don't need a bodyguard. Everything is normal—"

"Did you tell Sam about the hang ups in the middle of the night?" Louise asked.

"Yes. And for the record, I'm sorry I ever mentioned it to you guys," Jamie mumbled.

"If that were the only thing," Roy said, "we'd chalk it up to kids. But someone took her picture. I don't like it."

"Any idea who'd do that?" Sam asked.

Roy shrugged and shook his head. "Lunch and dinner are usually pretty busy at The Homestead. Anyone in town could have slipped in and out of this office without being seen."

"Or through the back door," Sam said.

"What?" Her father tensed.

"We walked right in the back," Sam explained.

Her parents looked at each other. "It's supposed to be locked all the time," Roy said.

"Maybe we've been a little careless about that," Louise admitted. "We'll be better. But your father is right. We don't like it. And just because you're not a little girl, that doesn't mean you don't need someone to look out for you."

Jamie sighed. "Look, you guys, I'm fine. You don't have to be concerned about me."

"It's what fathers do, sweetheart." Her dad gave her

shoulder a squeeze. "They watch over their children and make sure they're all right. Always."

Jamie happened to be looking at Sam and saw the "yeah, right" expression on his face. What did that mean?

"I know you can't help being protective, Dad, but I don't need Sam hanging around. The police checked everything out and there's no problem anymore."

"It's out of our hands," Louise interjected. "The auction is his community service."

"Thanks to Uncle Harry," Sam said dryly.

Jamie didn't want to debate that issue. "I'm sure there's another way for Sam to do his community service."

"It's a done deal," Louise said. "We paid the auction people already."

"That's right," Jamie said, snapping her fingers. "You bought and paid for him. How about he does his time working for you here at the restaurant? Maybe he can dust that empty frame for fingerprints and figure out who stole the photo."

"No way." Louise shook her head.

"Or he can beef up the security," she suggested.

"We bought him for you, sweetheart," her father said.

"What if I don't want him?"

"Way to make a guy feel warm and fuzzy," Sam said, one side of his mouth quirking up.

"She's not always so ungrateful," Louise apologized. "Usually she's gracious and considerate."

"Usually I don't have bodyguards showing up unannounced in my office," she said defensively. "Really, Mom, Dad—"

Suddenly Roy put a hand to his chest and began to massage the muscle.

"Dad? Are you okay?"

"Just a little pressure. It happens."

Sure it does, she thought. Her father was like the Rock of Gibraltar.

"He's not getting any younger," Louise said, looking worried. "And life is full of stress. Sometimes it's worse than others and you learn to deal with it. We found a way to help you and at the same time do some good for the town—"

"The town that lives up to its name," Sam cut in.

Jamie didn't miss the sarcasm. "Listen, you guys, just—"

"No," Roy said in his I'm-the-dad-and-this-is-the-last-straw voice. "You're young, Jamie. Your mother and I know what's best. We have more life experience. You moved away once, against our better judgment, I might add. We never liked Stu, but you wouldn't listen. And we weren't there to watch over you. And all you said when you moved home was that things didn't work out with him. So now you're back and we could watch out for you except you bought a house outside of town and you're all alone there." He took a breath as he continued to absently rub his chest. "Either you take Sam for the time we bought, or you move home and save your mother and me the stress of worrying that you're all right."

Her father was giving ultimatums. He did that when he got really upset, and Jamie felt a twinge of guilt. She *had* moved away to be with a guy she'd believed loved her and she'd done it in spite of her parents' disapproval. Turns out they'd been right about him. But she'd survived and picked up some of her own life experience.

She loved her folks, overprotective and all. She wouldn't hurt them for the world, but she simply couldn't move back home and start fighting for her independence all over again. She'd told Sam she wouldn't blink, but apparently she'd spoken too soon. Something had to give and apparently it was her.

"Okay. Bodyguard it is."

She met Sam's gaze and felt a flush on her face that spread clear through her. The thought of him guarding her body sent a shiver down her spine that was…excitement? Anticipation? Thrill? After the life experience she'd gained, she hoped and prayed it wasn't any of the above. Otherwise the next thirty days were going to be hell.

Chapter Three

Sam's headlights caught Jamie's tailgate full on, and for the second time that day he was following her and wondering what little Miss Litigation was doing driving a truck. She looked like a teenager who took daddy's wheels out for a joyride. Except, from what he'd seen, her father would have been copiloting that joyride. Sam had no frame of reference for her situation with her parents. Fatherly interaction had been noticeably absent in his formative years. The old man hadn't given a damn until he was dying.

As Sam continued to tail her along the dark, desolate road, he was beginning to think she was leading him on a wild-goose chase. Finally she made a right turn onto another dark, desolate road. About two miles farther, and he saw her brake lights as she pulled up in front of a house sitting all by itself on a dark, desolate piece of land.

"About damn time," he mumbled.

Then her truck door opened and out swung her legs, shapely calves and slender ankles. Between her interior lights and his headlights, he couldn't miss them—or the short skirt that rode up and revealed a hint of thigh as she slid out. Damn it. He could have gone thirty days without knowing this sassy, curly haired brunette had great legs. It was a visual he'd add to his list of things to forget.

"This is it," she said. "Home sweet home."

Her impractical high heels clicked as she walked up the four steps leading to her front door. She fitted her key into the lock and opened up the place. One glance over his shoulder at the dark and desolation made him realize what a sitting duck she was. He shook his head in disgust as he put his hand at the small of her trim back and urged her inside. Before you could say Buy-a-Guy, he'd closed and locked the door.

She set her purse and briefcase down as he looked around her living room and winced. If he'd never laid eyes on the owner, all the pink in this room would have screamed, Woman On Deck. No self-respecting guy would have a floral-covered sofa—leather and lots of it for him. But it wasn't all floral all the time. The two chairs were done in a geometrical pattern with the same colors of pink, beige and green. The room wasn't large, but there were enough wall hangings to choke a horse. And everything was neat as a pin. Windows had crisscrossed lace covering them so it would be very easy for someone to see in.

The entryway turned right, into the family room, so he followed it and flipped on lights as he went. The floor was beige tile, and a rose-patterned area rug sat in the center of the room. A green sofa and a chair were tucked away in the nook across from the TV, and a pass-through bar separated this area from the kitchen.

He went in there and glanced around, then opened the shutters above the sink to look out back. This whole place was vulnerable, but one look confirmed his worst fears. It was pitch-black outside and felt like there was nothing between her and the Canadian border.

"Do you have a security system?" he asked.

"No. It's not necessary. This is Charity City."

"I don't care if it's Sesame Street. You can't trust anyone. You live in the middle of nowhere, and the next neighbor is two miles down the road. Your attitude is dangerous."

She tipped her head to the side and looked up at him. "If I promise to be as cynical as you, will you go?"

"In thirty days," he agreed.

He walked back through the family room and heard her heels click, and then the sound was muffled as she crossed the rug behind him. Moving down the hall, he flipped light switches and glanced into bedrooms. The one with the computer, desk and bookshelf-lined walls was clearly a home office. A second had a twin bed with a fluffy comforter and treadmill opposite a thirteen-inch TV mounted on the wall—apparently a combination guest/exercise room. He wondered if Al Moore had ever been a guest and if so what kind of exercise they'd done. The thought didn't sweeten his disposition.

The last bedroom in the back of the house was obviously the master. A king-size four-poster bed with enough pillows for the Fifth Infantry dominated the center of the room. A floral-covered chair and ottoman sat in a corner with a dressing area and bathroom beyond. Pictures hung all over the walls, and more knickknacks filled space not occupied by photographs. He picked up the one of a familiar, smiling older couple. When he'd left Roy and Louise a little while ago their smiles had been full of relief and satisfaction that their plan had come together.

Those two had life experience, all right, and they'd just used it to work their miracle baby big-time. He replaced the framed photo on the dresser.

"So, that was the folks in action?" he commented.

"Welcome to my world."

"I particularly liked the pain-in-the-chest ploy."

But it was the zinger about her not learning from her mistake that had tipped the scales in their favor. Jamie had done something the folks disapproved of and it had come back to bite her in the fanny. His gaze automatically dropped to that portion of her anatomy. And a nice little fanny it was, he realized. Curves in all the right places.

"What I don't get is the part where they were afraid to tell you the truth."

"Afraid?" She folded her arms over her chest. "They're not afraid of anything."

"They're afraid for you."

"Okay, one for your side. But that's it."

"And the fruit doesn't fall far from the tree," he muttered. Hence her dangerous attitude. Some things she needed to be afraid of, and it was his job to show her.

"Are there any other outside entrances?" he asked.

"Why?"

So, she wasn't thrilled with the arrangement. That made two of them. But here they were. He gave her a look that had worked on some of the most hardened perps, but she didn't seem intimidated. He could respect that.

"Look, Counselor, just so we're clear, I can find out for myself. It would just save time if you'd cooperate."

"Okay. Let's be clear. I didn't ask for a bodyguard, but I agreed under pressure. That doesn't mean I'm onboard with this whole thing or that you can roll right over me in my own house. And while we're being clear, here's something else. I really don't know who you are."

That made two of them. He didn't know who he was anymore. And for the next month he wasn't free to find out. She took off her jacket and threw it on the bed, then turned her back and left the room. He hadn't realized she could move so fast in those high heels. They were at the front door before he caught up with her.

"Okay. I get it," he said. "You're not crazy about the situation. News flash, neither am I. But we're stuck with each other. The way I see it, things will go more smoothly if you follow some ground rules for the next thirty days."

"Twenty-nine," she snapped.

"I haven't been on the job a full day yet."

Although he wasn't sure why he felt the need to split hairs about that. The sooner he could get out of this town, the better.

"I don't particularly like your alpha-male, I'm-in-charge attitude."

"Meaning?"

"You can list ground rules from now until hell freezes over, but I'm not doing anything I don't want to do."

He decided not to argue that because she would find he *was* in charge. "I'm driving you to and from work. You clear your schedule with me and I always know where you are. Is that clear?"

"I understand the words, if that's what you mean."

"If you go to the ladies' room to put on lipstick, I want to know about it."

The stubbornness glittering in her eyes did amazing things to her particular shade of hazel. The obstinate expression canceled out the brown and gold and turned them to bright green. And beautiful. A man could lose himself in those angry eyes. He needed to avoid ticking her off, but somehow he didn't think she was the "go quietly" type.

She stared up at him. "Those rules strike me as overkill given that the calls have stopped."

"Your folks should get their money's worth."

"Unfortunately for you, they turned you loose on me and here are *my* rules. Assuming you actually stick around, you're not to interfere at work. No meddling in my personal life—"

"I'll need·to check out your boyfriend—"

"I don't have one," she said, her chin lifting a fraction.

What about Al, he wanted to ask. Instead he said, "Something wrong with the guys in Charity City?"

But he could answer his own question. Because his fist had a close encounter with Bo Taggart's nose, he was stuck with Jamie. In his opinion, there was definitely something wrong with the Charity City men.

"I'm sure there are some perfectly nice men in this town, but since I'm not interested in a relationship, I wouldn't know from firsthand experience." Her mouth pulled tight for a moment. "And remarks like that are exactly what I mean about not interfering. You need to be inconspicuous. No editorializing. Seen and not heard."

"Like a kid?"

"Hardly. You're no child. The deep voice and five-o'clock shadow are big clues." She huffed out a breath. "But I'm serious. If you insist on being underfoot, you can't disrupt my place of employment."

"No problem. At the office you're surrounded by the other lawyers—circling." Including Al. Jeez, he really didn't like that guy. And her frown told him she hadn't missed his deliberate, pointed pause. It was a not-so-subtle reference to the sharks that he believed attorneys to be. "You won't even know I'm there." When she rolled her eyes, he decided to let it slide. They were going to butt heads until this was over, and convincing her he could blend into her world wasn't a hill he wanted to die on today. "But your personal life is not hands off. In fact, no part of your life can be off-limits."

"That's unacceptable."

"I only know one way to do the job—thoroughly. You need to get that. The sooner you do, the easier it will be on both of us."

She put her hands on her hips. "This may come as a big shock to you, but I'm not especially concerned about making this easy for you."

"No?"

"No. I accepted this arrangement for my parents' peace of mind. Nothing more."

"They blackmailed you."

"Whatever. The thing is, I don't really expect you to guard me."

"Is that so?"

"Yes. In fact, I wish you'd simply go away." She opened the front door.

"Yeah. In a minute."

He turned and walked back through the house with the sound of her exasperation making him smile.

"What are you doing now?" She was right behind him. "Can't you just leave?"

"After I do a security sweep. I need to make sure all the perimeter doors and windows are locked."

When he was finished, they stood in the open doorway again and he backed onto the front porch.

"That was very thorough." Jamie looked puzzled.

"I warned you," he reminded her.

"I thought you had a problem with lawyers?"

"That doesn't mean I'm not going to do my job," he answered curtly.

His bad opinion of her profession was all about how cops took the bad guys off the street and lawyers put them right back on. His opinion about her? The jury was still out. But she stirred feelings in him that hadn't been stirred in a long time. He was sure he didn't like *that*.

"Still you're an overachiever on this bodyguard detail. Why?"

Good question. And another one he was going to ignore. "Sleep tight," he said, hearing the rasp in his voice. "See you tomorrow."

The porch light highlighted the pulse at the base of her throat fluttering wildly, telling him she was just as aware of him as he was of her. Imagine that.

"Tomorrow?" She shrugged, and the movement was anything but casual. "Guys don't always stick around." Her tone was full of challenge. "And the fact is, I wish you wouldn't."

After closing the door in his face, he heard the dead bolt. Good girl. Then the light went out and he was in the dark—in more ways than one.

He couldn't get the memory of her full lips out of his mind. A mouth that beautiful should be registered with the police department as a lethal weapon. Better yet, it should be against the law. Except, she was the law…and a living, breathing, walking, talking, knock-his-socks-off stunner who stood for everything he'd walked away from.

And if she could make him forget that in a few hours, what would happen in twenty-nine days?

The next morning Jamie hit her alarm clock three times before realizing the annoying noise was the doorbell. Squinting through the one eye she could manage to open, she noted that it was 7:00 a.m. Who in their right mind showed up on someone's doorstep at this hour?

Then her heart revved painfully. Maybe someone *not* in their right mind. A momentary fear gripped her before rational thought convinced her that if it was her mystery guy and he was up to no good, probably he wouldn't announce himself with the doorbell. Then she had another thought—scary in its own way. Maybe it was Sam.

That got her backside out of bed.

"Yeah. Right. Like he'll be back. Not," she mumbled.

She moved stealthily down the hall, then stopped where she could see out the front window without being seen. A black Mustang was parked out front. She breathed a sigh of relief before several shrill blasts of the doorbell made her jump. Then he pounded on the door a couple of times.

"Jamie? Are you in there?"

She threw the dead bolt and opened up. "Where else would I be?"

"Good question." He folded his arms over his chest as his gaze lazily wandered from the top of her bed hair, over her sexless, plaid flannel pajamas, to her red-painted toenails. "I guess it crossed my mind that you might've gone to work already. Without me," he added.

"And break the rules? Wish I'd thought of it," she mumbled.

The truth was she'd had trouble going to sleep. When she finally had, thoughts of Sam had kept her tossing and turning all night. Under normal circumstances she wasn't at her best in the morning. But after a horrible night due to abnormal circumstances, there was no doubt in her mind that she looked like twenty miles of bad road. And it bugged her that he looked like a brand-new superhighway.

He was wearing worn jeans and a white cotton shirt with the long sleeves rolled to just below his elbows. His hair was neatly combed and his lean face freshly shaved. No five-o'clock shadow in sight.

The thought made her cheeks burn as she recalled her immediate attraction to him yesterday. But today's reaction to him was no better. His deep voice and sexy, scruffy look was having a powerful effect on her. Dragging her eyes away from his she finally responded. "I didn't think of going to work without you because—"

"What?"

"I didn't think it would be necessary because—" She met his puzzled look. "I didn't think you'd actually come back."

"And yet, here I am."

In one large, attractive piece. And if there was a God in heaven, she hadn't said that out loud. And for crying out loud, where were her manners?

"Come in." She stepped back to let him walk inside. "I was just about to fix coffee and breakfast," she lied. "Want some?"

"Coffee? Or food?"

"Both."

"Can you cook?"

"I make a mean bowl of oatmeal."

"Gruel?" One corner of his mouth curved up. "Be still my heart."

Yeah, right back at you, she thought. "Is that a negative on breakfast?"

He shook his head. "It means I'll be cooking. If you have eggs."

"I do."

"That's my girl."

She stood by the door and watched his broad back disappear into her kitchen while her heart hammered against the inside of her chest. Shaking her head, she closed the door. How pathetic was she? Last night she'd lost sleep over Sam, and now her body was practically worshipping at his feet. The last time she'd done this it was all about the man she'd followed like a lemming to New York. And he'd used her before tossing her away when her body had done the inconceivable by conceiving.

After Sam disappeared into the kitchen, she heard

the sound of cupboard doors opening and closing. That was her cue to go to her room, splash water on her face and put on her ratty, sexless terry cloth robe. She didn't have any decent—make that indecent—lingerie. There'd been no need since she didn't have anyone in her life who'd appreciate it, and that situation wasn't likely to change.

Sam didn't count. Their association would be conducted only during business hours. That meant daylight. And temporary.

When she returned to the kitchen, he had coffee going, bacon cooking and bread in a toaster holding-pattern. Apparently his detective skills had served him well in finding what he needed.

"I'm impressed," she said, setting place mats on the table.

"About?"

"You. Cooking."

One eyebrow went up as he glanced over his shoulder. "You don't seem like the type who impresses easily. Should I be flattered?"

"No." She grinned. "Okay. You can be if you want."

"Smart-aleck."

"It's a talent." She set plates, silverware, water glasses and coffee mugs on the table.

"It looks good on you."

The compliment warmed her. Not that she'd been cold. Flannel, terry cloth and close proximity to sexy Sam Brimstone had kept her body's thermostat in the danger zone. If only she could chalk it up to being sleep deprived. But she had a bad feeling even if she got a solid, uninterrupted eight hours, her reaction would be the same.

When everything was ready, she handed him their plates to fill, then set them on the table. He waited for her to sit, then they started eating. After several minutes, lack of conversation became more than a companionable silence. Jamie wondered if it was her imagination that the air between them crackled with awareness and sexual tension. Or worse, was it wishful thinking on her part and she'd grown even more pathetic?

But after his crack about not knowing when a lawyer was finished, she'd be dipped in corn meal and fried up for Sunday supper before she'd be first to break the silence. So it went on until he'd cleaned his plate.

"How's the coffee?" he finally said.

"Good."

"You sound surprised."

"I guess I am. A man who can cook *and* make a good cup of coffee. How come no woman has snapped you up?"

"How do you know one hasn't?"

"No wedding ring for starters," she said, nodding toward his naked ring finger. "No tan line, either."

"Maybe I just don't wear a ring."

"Maybe. Yet you're going solo on a road trip. So if there's a Mrs. Sam, she's the most understanding woman on the planet."

He nodded. "Okay. You win. I'm not married. And

the hard-boiled detective cracks under rapid-fire cross-examination."

"Smart-aleck."

"It's a talent," he said, laughter in his eyes as he looked at her over the rim of his coffee mug when he took a sip. "Speaking of which, do you cook anything besides oatmeal?"

"Yeah. As long as it involves breakfast food. Dinner stuff? Not so much. Although you'd think since my folks own a restaurant I'd be more into it. But I guess that gene skipped me."

Needing something to occupy her hands, she wrapped them around her mug. This was different from her usual morning ritual. Normally her routine didn't include coffee and pleasant conversation with a man. Her kitchen table hadn't seen so much action in—well—ever. As tingly as she was from so short a time with Sam, she was glad the situation was temporary. She missed this part of being a couple. The intimacy. The not eating alone. But, because she could do without the breaking-up part, she embraced temporary with every fiber of her being.

"Were your parents disappointed when you didn't go into the family business?"

She wondered at his guarded look. Did he have an experience that had made him ask the question? Had he let someone down with his career choice?

"I don't think so," she said. "If they were disappointed about anything, I'd know about it. My parents aren't shy."

"Yeah. I noticed," he said wryly.

She laughed. "They always encouraged me to set high goals and do whatever I set my mind to."

"And being a lawyer was the highest goal you could set?"

Silly her for thinking they could have a pleasant conversation without him reminding her he had a beef with her profession.

"I have to get ready for work." She stood and took her plate to the sink. Stopping in the doorway, she turned and met his gaze. "I agreed to your presence, but that doesn't include allowing you to insult me."

"So noted. I'll do the dishes."

"You'll get no argument from me." And she left the room before he could remind her that arguing is what lawyers do.

Thirty-five minutes later Jamie was showered, dressed, coiffed and made up. When she met Sam in the tidied-up kitchen, he arched one eyebrow in surprise.

"You ready?" he asked.

"Yes."

"That must have set a land-speed record."

If he was trying to be funny and make up for his earlier remark, that was too bad. She wasn't ready to be over her mad. "I have to check my e-mail before we go."

Jamie didn't wait for a response. She went down the hall to her office and pulled up what she wanted on her computer. Quickly scrolling through her electronic messages, she determined there was nothing important—jokes, spam and advertising.

Just as she was about to shut down, something popped up on the monitor screen. Looking closer, she realized it was a digital photograph of her and Sam outside The Homestead. Judging by her clothes and the fact that she'd never laid eyes on Sam before yesterday, this picture must have been taken last night. That meant...

"Sam!"

He was there in a heartbeat. "What?"

"Look at this."

In the time it took for him to lean over her chair and let the spicy, masculine scent of his aftershave wash over her, he'd assessed the situation.

"We were followed," he said grimly.

"That's what I thought, too."

"And either this guy has your e-mail address or he hacked into your system. But I don't see any address for the sender."

"Me, neither." She glanced up and his expression made her ask, "What?"

"It would appear this guy's tactics have gone from lacking in originality, boring and clichéd, to high-tech." He gripped the back of her chair, and the look on his face frightened her. "Damn it. I shouldn't have left you alone last night."

Had the guy followed them here? As things kept sinking in, she shivered. "You didn't know we were being followed."

"That's the point. Never underestimate. But I did and it was a mistake. It won't happen again."

"You just said no one can know what he'll do."

"Yeah. But there's something I can do."

"Such as?"

"He just changed the rules and so will I."

"What do you mean?"

"Whether you like it or not, I'm moving in."

Chapter Four

Promptly at closing time, Sam walked into Jamie's office. Her secretary was just pulling her purse out of the bottom desk drawer. The thirtyish blonde struggled for a pleasant expression, something that didn't look so much like he was the scum of the earth for showing up at quitting time.

"Peggy," he said, glancing at the name plate on her desk. "I'm here for Jamie Gibson."

She studied him. "You were here yesterday."

"Yeah."

Now her blue eyes glowed with curiosity. "You're the bodyguard she told me about."

"Yeah."

"Then you don't need me." She pulled her keys out of her purse.

"Actually, I'll need to talk to you about—" The look she gave him said, Try to keep me past quitting time and you're dead meat. "But it can wait."

She nodded. "Good luck getting *her* out of here. She has no life except work."

If gainful employment was the criteria for a life, Sam had zero, zilch and nada. And he couldn't even *get* a life until he did his time here in Charity City. Ironic that his community service involved personal safety. He'd left L.A. in the first place because he was a complete failure at it. That's what happened when you promised something you couldn't do, like keep someone out of harm's way.

If he had an actual life, he'd give it up in a heartbeat to bring that woman back.

Sam watched the receptionist leave, then walked down the carpeted hall to find Jamie. Lights were on in some of the offices, but most were dark. Including Al Moore's—the creep. When he got to Jamie's door, he knocked once, then walked in.

She looked up and blinked at him, surprise flashing through her eyes. "You're here."

"Yup. As promised."

"But I'm not ready to leave yet."

"Maybe not, but it's time to go."

"You sound like my mother. Did she put you up to this? Is it a conspiracy to get me out of the office at a decent hour? Because my mother's been on my case about that for a while."

"Maybe you hadn't noticed, but I'm not exactly the motherly type."

Her gaze lowered from his face to his chest and she swallowed once. "Now that you mention it, no one would mistake you for a mom."

Good. Because it wasn't his job to worry about her long hours. But when their gazes locked again, he noticed the dark circles under her eyes—like twin bruises. In his line of work—make that former work—Sam had seen too many bruised women, too many unable to defend themselves. Violence happened to men, too, but they just weren't as vulnerable. And Jamie wasn't a big woman. She was delicate and small-boned and he didn't want to think about her in trouble. Hell, he didn't want to think about her at all.

"Sam, I still have work to do."

"Okay. I'll wait." He sat in one of the two chairs across the desk from her.

"Suit yourself." She turned away from him and mumbled something about being cooped up in the office all day thanks to him and still not finished with her work.

Was that thanks to him, too? Did he distract her? He didn't hate the idea.

When he drummed his fingers on the chair's arms, he watched her shoulders tense. Aha, he thought. She's not as hard-nosed as she pretends. So for the next ten minutes, he waged psychological warfare. She typed, he tapped. She printed, he fidgeted. As loudly as he could. With some serious sighing.

Finally, she swiveled around and glared. "Okay. You win. We can go. But I'm bringing work home with me."

He shrugged. "Whatever blows your skirt off."

Like that would happen even if she wasn't in a pant suit today. He missed seeing her legs, but nearly groaned out loud when she turned her back to him and bent to gather up her paperwork. The black slacks she wore showed off every sweet, rounded curve. It was true what they said, that what you couldn't see was pretty damned intriguing.

Sam had finally gotten her out of the office and nearly to her house before he acknowledged to himself that he hadn't thought through driving her to and from work. Since his Mustang was anything but a stretch limo, that meant he was in a confined space—with her. That meant soaking up the scent of her skin, his head saturated with the sound of her soft, slightly husky voice, and the sight of her lovely, graceful profile every time he glanced to his right.

Hell of a time to realize he liked his passenger seat empty. The loneliness was easier than this unwelcome attraction to the woman in it. The woman he'd promised to protect. She needed someone other than him, but he was all she had.

"Here we are." And about damn time, he thought, when his headlights picked out her house.

"Yeah." Her sigh was weary, and he almost felt the breath on his face.

His skin tingled as he stopped the car, grateful that he could put some space between them. He couldn't get out fast enough, but she was faster and was just starting up the front steps when he put a hand on her arm.

"I go first."

She tensed and met his gaze. "Oh. Right. After you."

When he held out his hand for her keys, she dropped them into his palm. He unlocked the door and, with Jamie right behind him, made his way through the place, turning on lights, checking doors, windows and closets and finally the answering machine. The light was blinking, and when she pressed the button, her hand shook slightly. But it turned out to be a message from her mother wondering how she and Sam were getting along. Just peachy, he thought, his fingers tingling as he studied the smooth skin of her flawless face. So much for space.

"When you call her back, tell her everything is secure for the night." He went back to the front door and heard her behind him.

"You're leaving?"

"Just to get my stuff out of the car."

"Oh. Right. Okay." She nodded and walked away.

Sam watched the sway of her slender hips until she disappeared down the hallway. The curvaceous counselor made him curious. She was no longer trying to get rid of him, in fact he'd swear she was relieved he was there. But clearly she hadn't expected him to show up this morning or after work. She wasn't very trusting, which maybe was good. But he couldn't help wondering who'd stomped the stuffing out of her faith in men.

He carried his duffel into the house and figured it went in the guest room. Sounds from the kitchen sent him in that direction where he found Jamie bent over the oven, sliding something inside. When she straightened and turned, he noticed that she'd changed into a Dallas Cowboys T-shirt that skimmed her waist and showed a hint of skin. Her worn jeans hugged the flare of her hips and the curves of her thighs, and the effect was like a sucker punch to the gut. He swallowed hard, instantly realizing that she was even more tempting in her All-American girl get-up than her professional suits. And he was committed to twenty-nine nights under the same roof with her.

This time it wasn't about not thinking it through. It was a matter of not making a mistake with her safety.

Dinner was hot dogs, sauerkraut, salad and fries. Damned if it didn't taste as good as anything he'd ever eaten. And he had a feeling it was about the counselor's company and not the cuisine. It was a replay of that morning, which he'd enjoyed more than he wanted. All except the part where his SOB streak kicked in and he ticked her off. But she hadn't let him get away with it. He liked that.

She dipped a fry in ketchup. "So what did you do with yourself all day while I was cooped up in my office?"

"I interviewed your folks and talked to some of your acquaintances."

"To see if any of them have a digital camera and know how to use it?" she asked wryly.

"Most cases are solved by basic, grass-roots, gum-shoe detective work."

"Because it's usually someone you know."

"Yeah." He couldn't help the urge to erase the worried expression from her face. "I would have talked to your receptionist, but she scared me."

"Oh, please." She laughed, just as he'd intended. "Peggy? A big, bad guy like you afraid of little Peggy Marsh?"

"She might be little, but it was quitting time, and when I hinted at an interview, she gave me a look that would strip paint."

"Don't worry. I won't let her hurt you."

"I'm going to hold you to that." He finished his last fry and leaned back in his chair. "Good dinner. You can add hot dogs and salad right under gruel on your extensive list of cooking accomplishments."

"Boy, are you easy."

He could be. The twinkle in her eyes was almost as seductive as her flannel pj's, because the underneath part is what counts. He'd had his share of women, some beautiful and some so so, and he'd found the heart and soul of a woman wasn't in the way she looked.

He stood. "I'm so easy, dish detail is mine tonight."

"I'll help." She picked up their paper plates and threw them in the trash.

"Wow. Don't hurt yourself."

"Not to worry."

She cleared the table while he loaded the few utensils and pots into the dishwasher. Standing in front of the sink, their gazes locked and he swore some electric current arced between them. This was not good.

"Look at the time," he said. "Probably you should turn in."

She blinked, then nodded. "Yeah. I wasn't expecting company, so the guest room's not made up."

She assembled linens and met him there, just across the hall from where she slept. She handed him sheets, blanket and pillow.

"It's a trundle," she explained, indicating the twin bed that looked a little short. "You can pull out the one underneath if you want. Together they make a king-size."

"Do you actually use that treadmill?" he asked, after setting the stack of linens on the bed.

"Yes. It's more than an accessory to hang clothes on. But I won't disturb you."

"Too late for that," he muttered, and hoped she hadn't heard.

"What?"

"It's getting late. You should turn in." He shoved his fingertips into the pockets of his jeans and leaned a shoulder against the doorjamb.

"Yeah." She hesitated, catching her bottom lip between her teeth. "Sam?"

"Yeah?"

"I know I gave you a hard time. But that pop-up

picture on the computer this morning kind of freaked me out. I'm glad you're here."

"Don't mention it. Now get some sleep."

But one last look at her mouth made him wonder about kissing Jamie Gibson. So this is what "between a rock and a hard place" felt like. His damn protective streak had landed him in Uncle Harry's courtroom, and too many days with Jamie was his sentence. Chalk one up for Uncle Harry. Way to make the punishment fit the crime.

"Thanks again." Jamie looked up at him. "If there's anything else you need, help yourself."

She hesitated just a moment before standing on tiptoe to kiss his cheek. He'd sensed what she was going to do a fraction of a second before she did it, and just before her mouth connected to his cheek, he helped himself to her lips. Her hands were on his shoulders for balance, but he took care of that when he pulled her against him.

The touch was like an explosion of fire, sucking all the oxygen from his lungs. Pressed against his chest, her breasts felt warm and soft and sweet. She smelled like a corner of heaven and her ragged breathing was music to his ears as he kissed the daylights out of her. And the moaning noise she was making in her throat nearly sent him over the edge of reason.

Nearly, but not quite. He had just enough sanity left to pull his mouth from hers and take a step back.

He blew out a long breath and backed up again as he gripped the doorknob until the metal cut into his palm. "That was unprofessional and should never have happened. For the rest of my community service, it won't happen again."

Jamie took one last look in the mirror and shook her head in disgust. She'd practically palette-knifed concealer underneath her eyes, and still the bags looked as if they would hold enough stuff for a trip around the world. Her folks might be resting easier, but her? Not so much. Now she looked like forty miles of bad road.

She felt like the princess and the pea. All night long she'd just known Sam was there. And just knowing rubbed her the wrong way because, God help her, she wanted to rub him. Run her hands over his chest. Feel the scrape of his five-o'clock shadow on her palms. Slide her fingers through his hair. Reliving that kiss. Hating herself because she'd liked it so much she'd have gone into freefall with him. But he'd remained cool, calm, collected and unaffected. Because he never wanted to do it again.

But she did. And that was going to make their close encounter of the mandatory kind a big problem. If only she could have talked her parents out of this whole thing. And Sam seemed determined to see it through, even though her uncle's sentence seemed excessive for what he'd done. That's it. There was one person she hadn't appealed to yet to get Sam off her back.

Maybe she could intervene with the judge and get him to reverse the sentence. She'd admitted to Sam that the pop-up picture had made her nervous, but there might be no way to find who was doing it. And when

Sam's community service was over, he'd be gone. She would still have to deal with her situation. She might as well start now—police, security system and Blackthorn Investigations. But first she had to see the judge.

She walked into the kitchen where Sam was waiting. "Ready to go?" she asked him.

"You haven't had breakfast."

She'd told him to help himself, and the clean dishes stacked beside the sink were evidence that he had. "I overslept. I'll get something later."

"Suit yourself."

They left the house and he escorted her to his car, politely holding the door open. When they reached downtown Charity City, she asked Sam to drive by the courthouse, which was across the street from Philanthropy Plaza.

"You're not going to the office first?" he asked.

"No. I need to talk to Uncle Harry."

He glanced at her. "Oh? He already threw the book at me."

"Yeah," she said grimly. "That's what I want to talk to him about."

"It's your breath to waste," he commented.

After he parked, Jamie led the way through the maze of courthouse corridors to the chambers of Judge Harold Gibson. When his court services officer recognized her, he waved her into the judge's office.

Uncle Harry looked up from the brief he was reading. He resembled her father—balding, round and always happy to see her. A wide smile split his face. "Hey, pumpkin. If it isn't my favorite niece."

She grinned. "I'm your only niece."

"Doesn't change how I feel." He stood and came around his desk to bear hug her. He let her go and looked at Sam. "Mr. Brimstone."

"Judge Gibson."

"To what do I owe this unexpected pleasure?" he asked her.

"It's about Sam's sentence," she began.

"Assault and battery is a serious offense." Her uncle tossed his glasses on top of the paperwork littering his desk. "Thirty days isn't out of line. And it could be jail time instead of community service."

"Look, Uncle Harry, we both know Bo Taggart is always hitting on unwilling women and probably deserved it."

"Probably."

"So you're going to let Sam slide?" she asked hopefully.

Her uncle shook his head. "Can't. For one thing he pleaded guilty to all charges. What kind of message would that send to the community."

"That you're fair and impartial?"

"Nope. I was thinking more soft on crime. And I'm not going there."

"I've seen you show mercy. Why not in Sam's case?"

"If I reverse my decision, every jackass between here and the panhandle will think it's okay to brawl in my town. And that's unacceptable."

Jamie put her hands on her hips and glared. "Is this about me, the auction and a bodyguard?"

"What makes you say that?"

"Because you're in cahoots with Mom and Dad."

Her uncle narrowed his gaze on Sam. "You can't go around assaulting folks. Fists are not the way to settle disputes. Jamie, of all people, you should know laws are in place for a reason."

"I do know," she protested. "But the court can show leniency at its own discretion. Sam shouldn't be stuck here because he gave a bully a taste of his own medicine."

"Stuck here?" Her uncle frowned. "Is there a reason you want him gone?"

Not *a* reason. She could come up with twenty and not even break a sweat. "No, it's just—"

The judge glared at Sam. "Did he get fresh with you?"

"No!"

Not much. And she started it. Sam was the one who'd finished it—once and for all.

She took a breath. "He's been a perfect gentleman, Uncle Harry. He even cleans up after himself."

"Good."

"But it bothers me that he hasn't been treated fairly. And by a member of my family."

"I'm sorry you feel that way, pumpkin. But I'm not going to reverse my decision."

"There's nothing I can say to change your mind?"

"Nope. But if it makes you feel better, your argument was first rate."

She gave him a hug. "It doesn't make me feel any better."

She said goodbye, and before they left, Sam shook her uncle's hand—like a perfect gentleman.

"Would it be out of line to say that stubbornness is a family trait?" he asked as they walked down the outside steps.

"I might have had better luck if you hadn't gone on record with a guilty plea. If you'd had representation, you probably wouldn't be in this fix. No attorney worth their salt would have let you plead this out."

"Next time I won't."

She slid him a wry look. "So you're planning to duke it out with Bo Taggart again? That's what we in the business call malice aforethought."

"If he didn't keep his hands to himself, yeah, I'd pop him again."

"Can I watch?"

He grinned down at her when he opened the car door. It was a good thing she had an invitation to sit or the sheer masculine beauty of his smile would have knocked her on her fanny. She couldn't deny that she was attracted to him. Or that her family had entrusted him with her welfare. But no way would she entrust him with her heart.

"Then I guess you better stay out of the Lone Star Bar and Grill."

"I'll do that." He rested his forearms on the top of the open car door. "If the Lone Star is off-limits, where would you recommend going for lunch in this town, pumpkin?"

Her eyes narrowed. "Smile when you call me that or I'll turn Peggy Marsh loose on you with her laser death look."

"Wow, you don't mess around."

Neither did he, more's the pity. "And don't you forget it."

"I won't. Or the fact that you tried to get me off the hook with your uncle." He slid his reflector sunglasses from the top of his head, down over his eyes. "So, where's the best place in town to eat?"

"The Homestead," she answered without hesitation. "And I'm not prejudiced. My parents' food is the best and they'll make sure the service is perfect."

"How about joining me?"

"What?" Surely she'd heard wrong.

"I'm asking you to lunch. My treat. It's the least I can do." He shrugged. "You tried to change the judge's mind."

"It was the right thing to do. You don't have to buy me lunch."

"Okay. Then how about letting me take you out because you were cooped up in your office all day yesterday—on my orders. Call it a reward for following the rules."

She gaped at him. There was no other word for it. And no words came to her mind, either. She could talk, spin or loophole her way out of any legal situation. And normally she'd have told him to put his rules where the sun didn't shine. But he'd caught her off-guard and she couldn't find a way to tell this man no. Even though that's exactly what she should do.

"Okay," she said.

"I'll pick you up at twelve-thirty."

And, God help her, she would look forward to it. But that didn't mean she'd changed her mind about men in general and him in particular.

Chapter Five

Sam sat across from Jamie at a table in a back room of The Homestead. It was lunchtime and the place was packed. Sam could see now what her father had meant when he'd said anyone could have taken his daughter's picture from the office at a busy time and no one would have noticed. But when it was how you made your living, busy was good.

And the food must be, too, or it wouldn't be busy. The Gibsons had successfully blended the western influence of Texas with fine-dining details. The walls were lacquered logs, and set in one of them was a big stone fireplace, black inside, a clue that it was actually used in the winter. The table was covered with linen tablecloth and napkins, and the center held a candle and bud vase containing an actual flower.

"I didn't see anything but the office the other night," he said. "Nice place."

Jamie glanced around, undisguised pride in her expression. "I told you. Wait till you taste the food."

Before he could answer, a young man appeared at their table.

"Hi, Miss Gibson."

"Kevin." Her smile was friendly. "Sam this is Kevin Phelps. Kevin meet Sam Brimstone."

Sam stuck out his hand. "Nice to meet you."

"You're her bodyguard?" the teenager asked, shaking hands.

"Yes."

"Cool."

"How's it going, Kevin?" Jamie asked. "How are you?"

"Good."

"How's school?"

"I'm graduating in a couple months."

"Congratulations. Good for you," she praised.

When she beamed a smile at the kid, Sam didn't miss either the way his neck turned red or the shy, self-conscious smile.

"So what are you going to do after graduation?" she asked.

"Charity City Community College. My grades could be better so I'm going to raise my GPA. Then I'll transfer to a four-year university as a junior."

"Good plan. So my folks can count on you for another couple of years?"

"You bet. I won't let them down. They took a chance, thanks to you putting in a good word for me."

"I'm glad I could help. Your mom must be proud."

"She is," he said, ducking his head again. "I'll tell her you stopped by." He slid a glance at Sam, which was two parts curiosity and one part animosity. Then he asked Jamie, "What can I get you to drink? The usual?"

"Iced tea would be great," she said.

"Make it two." When they were alone, Sam met her gaze. "What's his story?"

"I'm legal counsel for his mother, helping her out of a bad relationship. His dad has always been psychologically abusive, but the first time he hit her, she left. But it's hard on Kevin."

"Smart," Sam said, his thoughts turning to another woman who waited too long.

"But the man is still his dad. When the legal separation happened, Kevin started running with a bad crowd, not coming home and his grades went downhill. Then he was arrested while riding in a stolen car. Carol didn't know where to turn for help and came to me."

"How long was *his* community service?" Sam said wryly.

"Longer than yours." She unfolded her napkin and settled it in her lap. "The thing is, he needed direction and a way to fill the hours after school until his mom got home. My folks needed help here, so I brought everyone together."

"The arrangement seems to be working."

Better than his with her, Sam thought, staring at her mouth while want and need pooled deep in his gut. What would it take to get over wanting to kiss her again? A simple thank-you handshake would have sufficed, but no; she'd had to kiss him right after telling him to help himself to anything. Temptation got the better of his willpower. But it was just a moment. That couldn't cost him. Right?

Jamie pressed her lips together, almost as if she could read his mind. "It's working great as far as my folks are concerned. Kevin has been a loyal, trustworthy employee ever since he started here."

"Thanks to you."

She shook her head. "Thanks to the cops putting the fear of God into him at the same time he caught a break."

If only I could catch one, Sam thought. Along with being pretty, hot and tempting, she was modest. And a really good kisser. Which any detective worth his salt wouldn't know from firsthand experience, he thought grimly.

When Kevin returned with their drinks, he took food orders—Chicken Caesar for her, hamburger for him.

Then they were alone again, and she met his gaze. "I'm sorry I couldn't change Uncle Harry's mind and you're stuck here in Charity City."

That made two of them, he thought, watching as she drank iced tea, then licked excess moisture from her lips.

"It's life," he said.

"Were you going someplace important?"

Not unless you considered hell in a handbasket important. But he simply shrugged.

"Charity City is pretty far from L.A.," she persisted. "Seems kind of out of the way for you to stop in and say hi to Hayden."

"Yeah. That's not the way it started out. I got on Interstate 10 and drove east," he admitted.

"No destination in mind?"

"Nope." He rested his forearms on the table. "But the billboard on the highway caught my eye and I remembered Charity City was where Hayden moved."

She frowned. "And you walked into the Lone Star Bar and Grill just in time to give Bo Taggart a crash course in keeping his hands to himself?"

"Crash course." He grinned. "Very funny, Counselor."

"Thanks."

The corners of her mouth turned up, then into a full-on smile, and the wattage heated his blood and sent it sizzling through his veins to settle in points south. He forced himself to look straight ahead, but that was only marginally better. Her big eyes were full of green, brown and gold flecks that all added up to hazel. And beautiful. And then he noticed her frown.

Jamie unrolled her napkin and folded it in her lap. "You only wanted to see if it was the town that lives up to its name. But from your perspective, I guess it's a big disappointment."

"I didn't really expect advance billing to hold up. Usually doesn't."

"That's awfully skeptical. They say you can't judge a book by its cover or a town by first impressions."

He slid her an oh-come-now look. "Correct me if I'm wrong, but didn't I get a second impression from your uncle, the judge, just this morning?"

She sighed. "Why is it when things go wrong over and over, it's always the same person?"

"I think that's Murphy's Law. But you're the lawyer here, not me."

"I feel awful that your experience doesn't prove what a great place Charity City is to live and raise a family," she said regretfully.

"It's safe. Uncle Harry made it clear there's no brawling on his turf and he takes his responsibility to the town very seriously." He took a long drink of tea. "So why aren't you?"

She frowned. "Why aren't I what?"

"Having babies. Raising a couple kids."

The light went out of her eyes, and he wished for the words back. Somehow they'd hurt her, and he wanted to take her in his arms and make it better. But mostly he wanted to know what he'd said that made her look as if she'd lost her most precious possession.

She swallowed once, then seemed to pull herself together as she met his gaze. "In my experience it's best to build a solid relationship before taking things to the next level."

Which didn't tell him a whole hell of a lot. "What does that mean?"

"That I won't be having kids until—or unless—they have a father who will be there for them."

"Life doesn't come with a guarantee," he said cynically. When he met her gaze, it was filled with pain, and he put his own aside. "Does this have anything to do with what happened in New York?"

"It has everything to do with that."

"Do you want to talk about it?"

"No."

Just then their food arrived. Kevin politely inquired if there was anything else he could get them. When they said no, he left—after a longing look at Jamie, Sam noted. He felt something tighten in his chest, but refused to believe he could be jealous of a high school kid with impeccable timing. It was either a lucky accident or a deliberate cloak-over-the-puddle gesture. Either way, the kid had helped her past the awkward moment.

When her salad was half-gone, Jamie put down her fork. "So tell me about your family. Specifically your father."

"Taking a page from your book, I'd rather not talk about it."

"There was a great deal of bitterness in that 'life doesn't come with a guarantee' remark."

"Just a throwaway line. It didn't mean anything."

"Oh, please." She wiped her mouth with the cloth

napkin, then set it beside her plate. "You don't expect me to believe you were raised by wolves."

"No. By my mother."

"Is she still in L.A.?"

"No. She died about ten years ago."

"I'm sorry, Sam."

"Me, too."

"What about your father?"

"He's a bastard." The old anger welled up and tied his gut in knots.

"What did he do to you?" she asked, outrage shimmering in her eyes.

"He ignored me. Did I mention he's an attorney? When I decided not to follow in his footsteps, his interest in my life disappeared. He ignored my mother, too."

"I don't understand."

"Let's just say he wasn't a one-woman man. When she found out and refused to put up with it, he divorced her and took everything."

"That's too bad. The assets should have been split—or at least distributed equitably, plus child support. And what about alimony? Lots of times the party with the highest income is ordered by the court to pay the attorney's fees."

"None of that happened."

"Did she have legal counsel?"

He nodded. "For what he was worth. I tried to get her another lawyer, but she refused. The one she had was all she could afford and he caved at the first sign of a fight."

The law hadn't worked for her; it wasn't fair and equitable. His father's high-priced attorney had won every motion. But what bothered Sam most was that *he* hadn't been able to protect his own mother. Some people thought that made his choice of profession ironic, but he believed he was working hard to take the bad guys off the street. Eventually it had sunk in that lawyers were working equally hard at freeing those same bad guys.

"Well," she said, meeting his gaze. "I could get on my soapbox and do a couple hours on individual rights and protecting them. But that would be a waste of time. I can only tell you that I believe my job is about using my power for the powerless."

"Okay."

"I despise attorneys who make us all the butt of jokes and give the whole profession a black eye. Whether you believe me or not, I'm sorry about what happened to your mother."

"You don't owe me an apology."

"I know. But your father does."

"He's dead."

Her eyes grew wide, and she put her hand on his. "I'm sorry."

"I'm not. I'm only sorry that he left me a whole lot of money that should have gone to my mother. To make her life easier." He met Jamie's gaze. "I couldn't help her."

"I'm sorry, Sam." She squeezed his fingers reassuringly. "But I bet she'd have been proud of you. Being a cop. Helping people."

He didn't pull his hand away. Her touch felt too good. "I suppose."

"Why did you leave the force?"

He shrugged, then did pull his hand from hers and missed the warmth. "Burnout."

It was so much more than that. He was no good to anyone. All the victims he couldn't protect haunted him. Losing the one he was responsible for putting in harm's way was the worst. He didn't want to be responsible for Jamie, either. But due to circumstances beyond his control, he was. And he was afraid he would let her down.

Another hit to a soul already hemorrhaging.

"Thanks for the water, Mrs. Potts." Jamie handed one of the bottles to Sam and noticed the older woman eyeing the man who'd been living under her roof for the last three nights.

"You're welcome, dear."

Etta Mae Potts was silver-haired, small, seventy and had a mind like a steel trap, though the arthritis in her hands slowed her down. Still, she was the driving force behind the Charity City quilting society. Every month the ladies gave a handmade quilt to the local women's shelter and this time it was Jamie's turn to pick up all the donations.

With a gnarled finger, Etta Mae adjusted her wire-rimmed glasses. "You're sure I can't talk you and your young man into a piece of homemade apple pie? A bottle of water is not going to satisfy him."

"He's not my young man—" Jamie hesitated and glanced at Sam just in time to see the amused expression on his face. He was wondering how she would explain who he was and why he was tagging along today. She wasn't going there. "Thanks, anyway, Mrs. Potts. But we have to get back to town and unload all this stuff before it gets dark."

"Maybe next time." The older woman waved, then disappeared inside her small, red brick home.

Shoulders brushing, Jamie and Sam walked down the path to the street, and he opened the driver's-side door of the truck for her. He waited until she climbed inside, then shut it and rested his forearms on the frame. With the window down, their faces were inches apart.

Amusement lingered in his eyes. "How come I don't get a vote on that pie issue? Mrs. Potts will think your young man doesn't wear the pants in the family."

"Mrs. Potts would be right. And 'family' is stretching it, don't you think?"

"Depends on your definition of family." He walked around and hauled himself into the passenger seat beside her. "For the record, I'm starved."

There's a lot of that going around, she thought, inhaling the scent of his skin with its spicy cologne. The small smile curving his mouth reminded her of his heated kiss. And his muscular thigh was far too close to her own even though her truck did have a wide body.

Jamie turned the key in the ignition, and the engine

growled to life. "The sooner we unload all this stuff, the quicker you'll get fed."

After making a series of turns in the neighborhood, she guided the truck onto the highway and headed toward downtown Charity City.

"Seriously, Sam, thanks for your help today."

"There wasn't a lot of choice since I'm your shadow."

"You could have just come along for the ride."

His forearm rested on the open window, and the wind blew his hair. "And watched you fetch and carry and wrestle with all that heavy stuff? I don't think so. That's not the way I was raised."

No. Under difficult circumstances and without a positive role model, his mother had raised a gentleman. She glanced at him, then kept her eyes on the road. "If you'd been raised in Charity City, your mother would have had somewhere to turn when things got hard."

"What happens to all this stuff we picked up today?" he asked, a clue that he wasn't taking the bait to talk about himself again.

"It's going to a little store called Shade Tree which is right across the street from Philanthropy Plaza where it will be sold. The proceeds will be used to benefit the local women's shelter."

"Doesn't the shelter receive assistance from the auction foundation?"

"Yes, but not enough. The foundation helps a lot of causes, so that spreads the assets pretty thin. The shelter not only gives women and children a safe place to live, it offers programs to help them get back on their feet."

"Such as?"

"Job placement. High school equivalency tutoring. Even makeovers." She waited for him to ask.

"Why makeovers?"

She was only too happy to explain. "These women have been beaten down, physically and emotionally battered. Their self-esteem is pretty much nonexistent. Feeling good about themselves is a first step in reestablishing confidence. It's not at all about vanity. It's about rebuilding a life."

"How did you get involved?"

"At first I just represented some of the women in court. Helping them out of their situation legally."

"Then?" he prompted. He met her look. "I had to ask." He cocked his thumb toward the load in the truck bed and said, "This is a long way from getting someone alimony, then telling them to have a good life."

She shrugged. "I realized that a divorce decree is just the beginning for a lot of women, and I wanted to do more. So I do cases pro bono, and two days a month I pick up donations."

As they drove through town, she turned onto Benevolent Boulevard, then made a left into the alley behind Shade Tree. After turning off the ignition, she and Sam got out, meeting at the tailgate.

He looked down at her. "I don't know if Charity City lives up to its name, but you sure do live in the right town."

"It's like pebbles in a pond—the ripples drifting out from the center of impact." She rested a hip against the truck. "One of the auction stipulations is that if you benefit from foundation funds, you have to give back by donating time for sale. To keep it going. Shade Tree works that way, too. The women who get back on their feet give back by staffing the store, refurbishing the donated items if necessary, even trading child care when necessary so everyone can do their part. It's a win/win situation."

He shook his head. "Your parents neglected to mention this."

"What?"

"You're like an onion."

What? Was it her breath? "Them's fightin' words."

"That was actually a compliment." He pushed his sunglasses to the top of his head, revealing his eyes. "Like an onion, there are many layers that make up Jamie Gibson. As each one is peeled away, the new one revealed is even more fascinating."

"Wow."

"The thing is—I like you." His tone was reluctant.

The subtext: he didn't want to like her. And talk about layers. She stared into blue eyes that were so intense it was as if he could see into her soul. And he didn't hate her, which made her happy. So it was a good thing she'd given up men.

"Okay, then," she said. "I'll take it as a compliment."

"But you know what they say. No good deed goes

unpunished. And what you do for the shelter is classic good-deed material."

She didn't like the way he was frowning. "What's wrong?"

"As fascinating as this do-gooder thing is, it's another facet of your life I need to investigate. You said it yourself. Most crimes aren't random. They're committed by someone the victim knows."

A shiver raced down her spine, and she didn't like the reminder that she needed to be afraid. "I'm not a victim."

"And it's my job to see that doesn't change."

His job. She was nothing more than a job. And with every fiber of her being, she tried not to let that realization bother her. But his time left on the job was growing shorter every day. Surely it wasn't long enough for all his talk about fascination and layers and onions to get under her skin. But it was just long enough for her to be nervous.

Because she liked him, too, enough that she wouldn't mind if he kissed her again.

Chapter Six

Onions? Layers? He liked her? Sam wondered what he'd been thinking to tell her that. The truth was he hadn't been thinking—at least not with his head. He was acting like a hormone-riddled, junior-high poetry geek.

"Junior high was a walk in the park compared to living with Jamie."

He looked at his reflection in the bathroom mirror as he finished shaving and knew she was just across the hall in the shower. Naked. Wet. The double whammy. And his adult male hormones reacted accordingly.

After unloading her truck, the two of them had come back to the house and retired to their respective corners to clean up. It had been a long, dirty, sweaty and surprisingly satisfying day.

So she was a lawyer with a heart of gold—nothing like he'd expected.

And he'd blurted out the truth. At least part of it. The part he'd kept to himself was that the more he learned about her, the more he liked her. And the more tempted he was to break his promise and kiss her again.

But he wouldn't give in to the temptation.

After wiping off the excess shaving cream, he put on clean jeans and a T-shirt, combed his hair and braced himself to face an evening with Jamie. He found her in the kitchen making a salad, her back to the doorway so she didn't notice him. There were two steaks, seasoned and waiting to go on the grill. The kitchen table was set for two.

Couldn't have been more intimate unless he was making love to her.

The thought sent an instantaneous flash of heat to his groin. When she glanced over her shoulder and noticed him, he was afraid he'd groaned his frustration out loud. But her warm smile reassured him that his rampaging lust was still his secret.

"I don't have any homemade pie, but I thought steaks, salad, baked potatoes and biscuits would take the edge off your appetite."

"You thought right."

It was the sight of her bare feet with painted toenails that generated a surge of testosterone and kicked appetites of a different kind into high gear. She looked amazing in her worn jeans and snug T-shirt with the words It's Good To Be Queen stenciled on it. She'd pulled her hair into a ponytail and secured it on top of her head, letting the curls fall where they may. But they bounced in the sexiest possible way as she hustled around the kitchen. There wasn't a speck of makeup on her freshly scrubbed face.

He liked women, but he'd never wanted one so badly that need pulsed through him with an intensity that made him ache.

Sam cleared his throat. "I'll cook the steaks."

She looked up from slicing a cucumber. "You don't have to."

"I want to earn my keep." Translation: he needed to put distance between them.

"I'd say you did more than enough today. But if you want—" she nodded toward the back door "—the grill is heating up. Knock yourself out."

If only cooking would do it, he thought, but he was probably the classic example of "Out of the frying pan into the fire." Literally. Although he didn't think Jamie's grill could be much hotter than being alone in the kitchen with her.

He grabbed the meat platter and barbecue utensils and headed out the door. While the steaks were sizzling, he looked around. Bushes and yellow pansies surrounded her neatly manicured yard. An outdoor table, chairs and lounges were arranged on the patio. The space was serene, beautiful and intimate—just like its owner.

Wasn't that just dandy? So much for distance. She was with him wherever he went, and the distraction wouldn't help him do the job he was there to do. It just made things harder.

When the steaks were ready, he took them back in and set them on the table beside the salad bowl Jamie had placed in the center. There was a foil-wrapped baked potato on each plate.

"Mmm. Smells good," she said.

Not as good as you, he thought. This had to stop. He could not get personal and do justice to the job he was supposed to be doing.

"I think we're ready. Let's eat."

Sam sat where she indicated and poured all his frustrated energy into his meal. Somehow he had to find a way to get back his objectivity, his professional facade. He had to reassert his detachment. Treat her like anyone else in a case he was investigating. And when he was involved in a case, he asked questions. So that's what he would do now.

He cut a piece of beef and looked at her. "So, are you ready to tell me what happened in New York?"

"No."

"Any particular reason?"

"I haven't told anyone."

"Not even your folks?"

"Especially not them."

"Why's that?"

"So many reasons," she said, wiping her mouth with a paper napkin.

"Gimme a for instance."

"To protect them."

Sam met her gaze. "News flash. I'm not them. And I don't need protecting. But I do need information. About you. Anything that will help the investigation," he added, wincing when his voice grew raspy.

"New York is ancient history. There's nothing about it that's relevant now."

Baloney. It might not be relevant to the case, but she still had unresolved feelings. And since when did he think like a shrink?

"Why don't you let me be the judge of what is or isn't important," he said.

She sipped iced tea as she met his gaze, her own frankly assessing. "You're not going to back off on this, are you?"

"No."

She thought for a moment, then nodded. "Okay."

"So what was the guy's name?" Might as well start simple.

"Stu. We met and fell in love in law school." She sighed and pushed her plate away, leaving half her dinner. "At least I was in love. He did a convincing imitation."

"Did your parents meet him?"

"Oh, yeah. It was dislike at first sight."

"Given their inclination toward overprotectiveness, that's not breaking news."

She shook her head. "They're not protective about guys anymore. In fact, they can't wait for me to meet someone and get married so they can turn over the day-to-day responsibility for my well-being and stop worrying about me."

Sam could relate. "So how did you end up in New York?"

"Stu was very persuasive that working for a firm there would look good on a résumé. He convinced me to go. Over my parents' strenuous objections, I might add. It didn't take all that long to find out they were right about him."

"What happened?" he asked, pushing his own plate away.

She was shredding her napkin. "He said we'd be together forever, that nothing could tear us apart. But we were only there about six weeks when I found out I was pregnant."

"A baby?"

"That's what pregnant means," she said wryly. "I was going to have a baby."

In his LAPD days he'd heard it all and thought nothing could shock him. But somehow her revelation did. And he was a pretty good detective, but it didn't take a whole lot of skill or psychic ability to know something bad had happened, because she didn't have a baby now.

"How did Stu take the news?"

"He split."

"What?"

"He left. Walked out. Dumped me."

"Son of a bitch…"

Her hands stilled and her gaze grew distant as she quietly said, "When I lost the baby, I was all alone."

"Why?" He didn't know what to ask, what to say—how to take away the shadows swirling in her eyes.

"It was sudden. It was New York. I'd just started a new job and didn't know anyone very well. Stu was gone and not picking up his cell that night. My parents were too far away."

"What did you do?"

"I went to the E.R. in a cab."

Sam thought he'd been angry when he'd gone into the Lone Star and saw Bo Taggart groping that waitress. It was nothing compared to the rage he felt now. He'd give anything for five minutes alone with Stu—the son of a bitch—no questions asked.

"Say the word," he growled. "I'll track him down and beat him up for you."

Her surprised gaze jumped to his. Then she shook her head sadly. She stood and took their plates to the sink, then came back to the table.

"As appealing as that thought is, it could mean more community service for you, and you've already got more than you should on my behalf."

"I'll risk it."

She was trying to make light of it, but he was only half joking. And when he saw the tears in her eyes—for the baby she lost, for going through it alone, for keeping it inside all this time—he couldn't stand it.

At that moment all his warnings about professional,

personal and putting distance between them went out the window. He couldn't stand seeing her look like that. Taking her hand, he tugged her onto his lap and into his arms. Jamie stiffened for a moment, then curled against him and buried her face in his neck, letting go of the tears she'd held back. All he knew to do was hold her, rub her back and whisper meaningless words. None of it was enough to fix what pained her.

Because she was in his arms, he felt her struggle for control. He was doing the same dance—but for a different reason. All her soft curves pressed to him would tempt a card-carrying saint. And he still had that SOB thing going on.

She sniffled, then lifted her head and looked at him, her big green eyes looking bigger and greener because they were red from crying. "Sorry, Sam. I'm sure comforting a weepy female isn't in a bodyguard's description."

"No. But your welfare is part of the job. And it's better for you to get that out. I'm still surprised your folks don't know."

She sighed as he took her hand and rested their linked fingers on her thigh. "Unlike the cooking gene, I guess I did get the overprotective one. I kept the details to myself. The story for public consumption was that I got dumped and I was coming home. Mom and Dad were just happy about that and fortunately didn't ask too many questions."

"Not like me."

"Yeah." Her eyes filled again. "Bet you won't do that again."

There *was* something he shouldn't do again, and it was worse than asking questions, but he couldn't find the will to stop. He took her face in his hands and touched his lips to hers, tasting salty tears and the lingering sadness and pain. Her palms slid up his chest and over his shoulders, settling around his neck as he captured her sigh of surrender with his mouth. He traced her lips with the tip of his tongue, and when she opened to him, he took what she offered, needing to be closer.

What was meant to comfort quickly turned into a rush of excitement that was hot and bright and consuming. She was so soft, so sweet, so good. How could anyone walk away from her? How could anyone hurt her?

The thought was like a bucket of cold water in the face. They were both breathing hard when he put his hands on her arms and gently tugged them from around his neck. Surprise burned away the glaze of passion in her eyes.

He blew out a long breath. "Jamie, I'm—"

"Don't say sorry." She shook her head. "Please don't. I'm not sorry. I wanted that to happen. I like you, too, Sam. And I'm not happy about that any more than you are." She stood up and backed away. "But for the next few weeks, we have to find a way to deal with this."

Then she walked away.

Sam jammed his fingers through his hair as he sucked

in air. That's what he got for asking questions. He'd thought it was best—a way to get back on track. And it turned out he got more off track than before. Jamie was right. He had to find a way to deal with it.

She'd been hurt, but her heart would mend. As long as she stayed safe. She needed the best to keep her that way and he'd just proven he wasn't it.

Jamie glanced over her shoulder to make sure she wasn't followed, then opened the heavy door at the Lone Star Bar and Grill. She'd declared a level-orange emergency when she'd called her friends—Abby Walsh, Molly Preston and Charity Wentworth—and asked them to meet her here. As she passed a leering Bo Taggart, she kind of wished she hadn't given Sam the slip. But she needed help *because* of him, making his presence a problem, which was why she'd specifically chosen this location.

When she spotted the girls at a corner booth, she quickly made her way over and sat down beside Charity. A waitress walking by stopped and took their drink orders.

Then Jamie let out a long breath. "Hi. Thanks for coming, you guys."

"So why are we here?" Abby tucked a strand of straight brown hair behind her ear and wrinkled her nose in distaste at the scarred wooden floor with discarded peanut shells scattered over it. "I miss The Homestead."

Jamie followed her gaze, then noticed stuffing poking through rips in the plastic seat and carving on their table that read For a good time call Wanda.

She sighed. "We're here because this is the last place Sam would come looking for me."

"If you weren't my friend, this is the last place I'd be." Molly, the redhead of the group and sitting across from her, slid closer to Abby when Bo walked by and gave them the once-over followed by a come-hither smile that made them cringe collectively.

Jamie looked at them. "I needed to talk and you guys are my best friends. If any one of you needed me, I'd be there in a heartbeat."

Beautiful, blond Charity Wentworth, their society buddy, glared at Bo's back. "Why won't Sam come here? Besides the fact that he's very good-looking, having his muscles in attendance would make me feel a whole lot safer."

Depends on what kind of safe you were talking about, Jamie thought. She trusted him to keep her from physical harm, but he was heartbreak waiting to happen. How safe could that be?

She gave them the Cliff's Notes version of the harassment, and her parents buying Sam at auction after her uncle had mandated community service.

Abby frowned. "We've all met Sam. He interviewed us about this guy who's bugging you. And I don't understand why you came here without him. Especially with some wacko sending pop-ups on your computer."

"First of all," Jamie said, "I was very careful when I took a cab from the office."

Charity's expression turned dreamy. "Still, it must be nice having all those muscles on your side." She nodded at her friends approvingly. "In fact, all of you ladies purchased some fine-looking men at the auction."

"I have a small but relevant point," Jamie said. "I didn't buy Sam. Mom and Dad did, and he's driving me crazy."

"Join the club," Abby and Molly said together.

Then they looked at each other and laughed. Just then, the waitress dropped off their orders.

Charity sipped her white wine and made a face. "I just know this came out of a box." She looked at Jamie. "But a friend in need… So there's crazy. And there's crazy." Her voice dropped into the sexy range on the last word which meant man/woman kind of weird. "Which one is Sam?"

"The second one," Jamie answered on a sigh.

"Did he kiss you?" Abby demanded.

"Twice." Jamie felt no satisfaction at rendering this group speechless. But their collective jaws dropped. "The first one, technically, I started. But Sam took it to the next level."

"You lawyers," Molly said, shaking her head. "Always spinning a situation. That's what I like about my preschoolers. They say what they mean. Direct and to the point."

"I know what you mean," Abby agreed. "This is like trying to get the facts from my high school kids. Not easy to do when my library is a hotbed of hormones. So, Jamie, give us the truth, the whole truth and nothing but the truth."

"So help me God," she said. "I was just going to kiss his cheek."

"Why?" Charity demanded. Smoke from the booth behind them drifted over and she waved it away with her hand.

"That doesn't matter. But just before I connected, he intercepted my mouth with his mouth."

"How was it?" Charity asked.

"His mouth should be registered as a lethal weapon with the romance police."

"Ooh," all three said together.

"The second time," Jamie said, "it was all him and even better than the first time."

"Then what?" Molly asked, tucking a strand of red hair behind her ear.

"He said he was sorry. At least he started to."

"Ouch." Charity's expression was sympathetic.

"Do you like him?" Abby asked.

"Yes." Jamie didn't tell them Sam had admitted he liked her, too. She just didn't want to go there, where her good friends would put a positive spin on the situation. Where they tried to convince her she could find happiness with him. She'd found out there was no such thing, and now she was through with men. "I know very little about him. He left LAPD and he doesn't have much use for attorneys. But Hayden Blackthorn spoke highly of him."

"Hmm." Charity tapped her lip with a long red fingernail.

Molly pointed. "Something tells me your Sam is the dark, dangerous type."

"And that type is hell on a girl's heart," Charity said.

"He's not *my* Sam." Jamie rubbed a finger across the carving in the table. "Besides, he's just passing through."

"No chance he'd reconsider when he's finished with community service?" Charity wanted to know.

"Nope."

Jamie didn't believe in clinging to false hope. Sam *was* leaving town. She knew that. And she'd always believed knowledge was power. But the power of his kiss had weakened her defenses, and she wasn't so sure she would get through his community service unscathed.

"Good evening, ladies."

Jamie started at the familiar, deep, masculine voice, but did a double take, anyway. "Sam!"

"Counselor."

Even in the dim light of the sleazy bar she could see that his jaw bunched and she could probably bounce a pebble off the tension radiating from him. "How did you find me?"

"The same reason you picked this place."

"Because it's the last place Sam would come looking for you," her friends said together.

"He *is* good," Charity added, giving him an approving look. "Join us, Sam."

And, damn it, he did.

* * *

During the drive from the Lone Star, Sam didn't say two words to her. He was too ticked off. When he stopped the car in front of the house, he let out a small sigh of relief for the first time since discovering her gone. *That* had royally ticked him off.

He got out of the car and went around to the passenger side to open the door. "So you want to tell me what that was all about?" he demanded.

She slid out, and the interior light emphasized the dark circles under her eyes. "I have a standing date with my friends."

Anger rumbled through him. She couldn't quite meet his eyes, and he knew that was a stretch of the truth but decided not to push the point. "What about the rules?"

"I needed some breathing room," she said, her stubborn little chin lifting defiantly.

That was completely his fault. Because he'd kissed her. The jerk in New York had hurt her, so she'd responded to his kiss with fight-or-flight mentality. And she'd picked the latter. If anything had happened to her, the blame would be squarely on him.

"You put yourself at risk," he said, stating the obvious.

"In a couple weeks you'll be gone and I'll be coming and going on my own, anyway."

She was right.

When he didn't respond, she headed for the front porch where Sam had left the light on.

It wasn't now.

In two strides he caught up to her and grabbed her arm. "Wait."

It was too dark to see her expression, but Sam felt her tense. The lamps inside were still lit, so maybe the exterior fixture had simply burned out. Jamie unlocked the door and when he opened it, light from inside revealed that the bulb hadn't simply burned out. It was missing. And he saw something else that knotted his gut.

Bending down, he picked up a standard, letter-size envelope. He pulled out the photos tucked inside and stared at them as tension knotted his gut. They'd probably been taken with a digital camera in the last couple of hours. Pictures of Jamie and her friends at the Lone Star Bar and Grill.

Jamie met his gaze, and her own was wide with alarm. "He followed me."

"Yeah," he said grimly. "Then he got one step ahead."

Sam hustled Jamie into the house and kept her close while he checked it out thoroughly. There was no evidence that whoever left the pictures had been inside. That was the good news. The bad—they were no closer to identifying the creep. And he came to a couple of conclusions real fast.

The harassment was escalating, and he couldn't let Jamie out of his sight. If this guy didn't make a mistake, show himself, soon . . . Damn it. He was running out of time to find the threat and neutralize it.

He put his hands on her arms and forced her to look at him. "Okay, here's how it's gonna be. From now on you're working from home where I can keep you safe. This isn't negotiable. No dinner with girlfriends. No giving me the slip. No unauthorized trips anywhere. No—"

"I get it, Sam," she said quietly. "I'll work from here."

He dropped his hands, and the realization hit him. He'd just gotten her to agree to his terms. In reality, the last thing he wanted or needed was the sweet torture of more one-on-one time with Jamie. His level of concern for her told him something else. This wasn't a job anymore.

It was personal.

Chapter Seven

When she'd agreed to work at home, Jamie thought, she'd had no choice. But she wasn't used to working with Sam around. He was a distraction, and that was an understatement.

She'd phoned the office first thing that morning, and after an explanation, they'd messengered over the requested files. After breakfast she and Sam had come in her home office to work. She was at her U-shaped desk facing him where he sat at a card table, poring over files of cases she'd been involved in for the past year. She was trying to concentrate, but every time she glanced up, there he was in his T-shirt and jeans. It wasn't fair. No guy should look that good in an old pair of denims and an ordinary shirt.

When her gaze once again strayed from her computer monitor to his broad shoulders and then his face, she noticed the frown and deep creases of worry between his brows. Her heart did a funny little skip when it dawned on her that he was concerned. About her.

With good reason, she thought, shivering at the memory of the photos on her doorstep last night. And her night out alone with the girls had made his job harder.

"I'm sorry, Sam."

He looked up. "What?"

"About last night—not telling you where I was going. I never said I was sorry. I'm saying it now."

He rubbed a hand across the back of his neck. "It could have been worse."

"I get that now," she said, and shivered though the room was far from cold. A byproduct of working with Sam.

"Then it was a cheap lesson." He closed the file in front of him and set it on the stack beside him before opening another one.

"So what are you looking for?" she asked.

He glanced up again. "I don't know."

"Then why go through them?" She rested her elbow on the desk and settled her chin in her palm.

"Because something might jump out at me, and right now I've got nothing to find this guy. The average person today is computer savvy and has the skills to use a digital camera. It was child's play to send you a computer message without leaving a trail and even easier to photograph you and your friends, then make prints and set them on your porch without a clue for us to go on."

"But my files are like looking for a needle in a haystack. Do you really expect to find something there?"

She should stop talking and let him do his thing, but for some reason words kept coming out of her mouth. To get his attention? She didn't want to believe it but there was nothing to be gained by burying her head in the sand. That just left her backside exposed. True, he was a distraction. But the truth was she liked his deep voice. She liked having someone to talk to, and looking at him stole the air from her lungs—but in a good way. All of that added up to the fact that she liked having him there.

"Maybe," he said, rolling his shoulders as if they hurt from too long in the hunched-over position. "Maybe not."

"But maybe the perp is someone the victim knows. Victim," she whispered, and couldn't help shivering again.

"Nothing's going to happen to you."

Not on my watch, his look said. Only, his watch was growing short. "So I know you want me to work from home because it makes personal safety easier. But why did someone have to bring me the files? You could have come with me to the office."

"The pictures are proof that he knows where you work and where you live. But it's not like this is a bustling metropolis. He can't blend into the burbs here. My guess is your office is his starting point. Where he keeps tabs on you."

"And?"

"If he doesn't see you there for a while, he'll be forced out of his comfort zone and make a mistake."

"And we grab him," she agreed.

"Actually, *I'd* be doing the takedown," he said, his tone wry.

A glance at his wide chest and muscular arms was enough to convince her he had the goods to back up the words.

"Thank you, Sam."

"For what?"

"Everything," she said lamely.

"You can do better than that, Counselor."

"Okay. Your efforts are above and beyond the call of duty for a man who was railroaded by the Charity City legal system. And I appreciate it."

"You're welcome." His mouth turned up at the corners.

A warm feeling started in the pit of her stomach and spread outward. He was committed to keeping her safe, and the idea didn't make her want to run screaming from the room. The bigger question was why? After what had happened with Stu, she was determined to do her own thing, make her own decisions and generally live her life independent of a man.

But this particular man had efficiently clipped her wings, and she'd just thanked him for it. What was that about? She liked having him there, but that was different from needing him. She wouldn't let herself need him.

"So can we talk about what happens when your servitude to the legal system is complete?"

"What do you mean?" He frowned.

"Like I said last night, when your time is up, I'll have to deal with this problem. I can't stay locked away here forever."

Although, it was a tempting thought, if he was there with her. Nope, she thought, catching the slip. Absolutely not going to need him.

"I'll catch the guy."

"But if you don't, I'll have to put some other protection in place."

"There's time. First let me concentrate on figuring out who this bastard is."

"Okay."

She tried staring at her computer monitor, hoping if she did so long enough, her brain would kick into work mode. It didn't. She could smell the spicy scent of Sam's aftershave, and it did a number on her brain function. He didn't seem to have the same problem, she noticed, as he studied the file in front of him. He might have been the sole inhabitant of another planet for all the notice he took of her. While it didn't pump her self-esteem, there was something to be said for that level of intensity and focus.

Jamie wondered what it would be like if he kissed her again and channeled those considerable skills into mouth-to-mouth stimulation. The thought made her shiver again, and not because she was scared. How pathetic was she that she'd be a willing participant in seduction initiated by a man she knew was leaving town?

But as Sam rubbed his chin and turned a page in the file, Jamie figured it was good that his powers of concentration were engaged for her own good. Neither one of them wanted to get personal, but she couldn't help being curious about this man. It occurred to her that those same powers he was using on her behalf probably made him a better-than-average detective. He wanted to help people and he was good at it. Which begged the question: Why had he quit the police force?

She'd asked him once but he hadn't answered. Her gaze narrowed on him. He wasn't the only determined one.

"Sam?"

He looked up. "Hmm?"

"Why did you leave the LAPD?"

He closed the file and set it on the growing stack beside him. "It was time."

"Since you're clearly too young to retire, that's not a satisfactory answer."

"Don't you have work to do?" he asked, folding his arms over his chest.

"Yes. But that's also nonresponsive."

"And your point?" he snapped.

The tone was meant to put her off, to intimidate, but he didn't scare her. Stalker boy with the photo fetish terrified the living daylights out of her, but Sam Brimstone? Not so much.

"You're focused and determined, two qualities that I'm sure made you an extraordinary detective. And I think you loved it. So what's your deal?"

"What does it matter?"

"I want to know."

"Do you always get everything you want?"

"No. If I did, I wouldn't have lost my baby."

"Jeez, Jamie. I didn't think—" He rubbed both hands over his face.

She wasn't sure why she'd said that, why the words popped out of her mouth. Probably telling Sam had stirred up all the feelings she'd suppressed. But there was no way to bring her child back. She had to move forward. And, surprisingly, the pain of remembering wasn't as bad as before. But this wasn't about her. She stared him down without blinking.

Finally he let out a long breath. "Okay. You win. And you're right. I was a pretty good detective."

Jamie would put money on the fact that he still was. "And?"

"I usually got whoever I went after."

She didn't doubt that and made up her mind not to be someone he went after. "I hear a but."

He ran his fingers through his hair then met her gaze. "But I couldn't always keep them behind bars. Legal loopholes. Circumstantial evidence wasn't always enough for a jury, and my gut feeling about a perp's guilt wouldn't get a conviction. Then, even if the evidence added up and we had all our ducks in a row, the defense would go after police procedure."

She understood his frustration. "The system isn't perfect, but it's all we've got," she said quietly.

"Yeah. I get that. But one day it just felt like the bad guys were the only ones winning, and I walked away."

The look on his face said there was so much more he was holding back. She got up and walked around her desk, stopping beside him to put her hand on his shoulder. He flinched as if she'd burned him, then reached up and covered her hand with his own.

When he met her gaze, she said, "But, Sam, if everyone stops trying, the bad guys will win for sure."

"It's not my fight. So I got in my car and started driving."

And stopped in Charity City because the billboard caught his eye. Soon he'd get back in the car and start driving again. She'd known that from the beginning, but this time the realization made her chest hurt.

Now that she'd had this interlude of 24/7 togetherness with him, Jamie wondered how much more it would hurt when he walked away.

Sam knew Jamie was right about putting protective measures into place when he was gone. And he didn't want to think about the fact that leaving Charity City wasn't quite as appealing as it had been a few weeks ago. Right now he was meeting with Hayden Blackthorn.

"Nice place," Sam said, looking around his friend's home office.

Sitting behind his desk, Hayden was leaning back in his chair, fingers linked over his flat abdomen. "You haven't seen the whole place."

"What I have seen is pretty impressive."

Sam remembered being damned impressed when he'd driven up the long drive to the imposing, redbrick mansion—or more accurately, castle. But he'd found Texas houses were like that. Big. Imposing. On his way through the house he'd had an impression of space, expensive furnishings and luxury. Now they were in an oak-paneled office and he was sitting on the other side of the desk in a cushy, leather wing chair.

Hayden leaned forward and rested his forearms on his paper-littered desk. "It's about time you came to see me. I heard from Roy and Louise Gibson that you were in town."

"I've been a little busy," Sam said wryly. "Did they tell you why they wanted a character reference?"

"Yeah. How's that going? Any leads on Jamie's weirdo?"

"No. And the behavior is escalating." Sam explained what had happened and that he'd insisted Jamie work from home.

"You think she's in danger." It wasn't a question and Hayden's expression turned grim.

"I never rule it out." Not anymore. The familiar stab of guilt pricked him.

"I see. So if you're supposed to be guarding her, where is she now?" Hayden asked.

"I left her with Riley Dixon. She's picking out a home-security system. He's got orders to keep her there until I come back."

"He's a good man." Hayden met his gaze. "So why do I get the feeling this isn't an entirely social call?"

"Because it isn't."

"Tell me what you need."

Sam needed to feel nothing for Jamie and never to have kissed her. He needed to turn back time and protect a woman from the man who was determined to possess her, determined that no one else would have her. But he couldn't turn back time or change the fact that he'd let both women down. So far Jamie hadn't paid too high a price. And he was here to see that she didn't. He was leaving and she would have to deal with her situation.

But not on her own.

Sam leaned forward and rested his elbows on his thighs. "I want to retain Blackthorn Investigations. If I can't nail the bastard, Jamie's going to have more than just a home-security system when I leave."

Hayden nodded. "I can assign someone for personal protection and continue the investigation."

"I was hoping you'd say that."

"We can work out the details when—and if—it becomes necessary."

"Good." Sam let out a breath. "And another thing."

"Whatever you need."

"Send the bill to me."

"You going back to L.A.?"

"You worried about getting paid?" Sam returned.

"I'm worried about you. I know what happened," Hayden admitted.

Sam's gut knotted. "How?"

"When I heard you were in Charity City with too much time on your hands, I checked it out. It's what I do and I still have a lot of contacts in L.A."

"How is your brother?"

Hayden flinched. "I wouldn't know. Probably still a back-stabbing bastard. But you're changing the subject."

"You noticed. I did that because there's no point in talking about it. Past history. Water under the bridge. Over."

"Are you trying to convince me or yourself?"

"It's a fact."

"And the fact is, talking it out would—"

Sam glared at him. "It won't bring her back."

"What happened isn't your fault, Sam."

"Yeah, it is. I thought I had all the answers."

"That's not a hanging offense." Hayden's voice was quiet—firm but gentle. The same tone he used with his daughter.

As if reading his mind Sam said, "How's Emily?"

Hayden sighed. "Okay. You win. We won't talk about it." He smiled. "My daughter is fine. My mom took her to the mall. Clothes shopping."

"Does she miss her mother?"

"We both do." His mouth thinned to a grim line, no doubt remembering the woman he'd loved and lost in a car accident.

"Does Em like it here in Charity City?"

"Yes." The dark look disappeared. "I do, too. It's a great place to put down roots. Raise a family."

"So I've been told."

By Jamie. Sam knew now why she'd looked so sad when she'd said it. And he'd lived up to his initials yet again when he'd asked if she always got everything she wanted. She'd wanted her baby. To raise a family. Except the jerk messed her over. For reasons Sam didn't get, she'd told no one but him about what had happened. Did that mean she had faith in him? If so, he needed to make sure she knew her trust was misplaced.

Hayden shifted in his chair and crossed one ankle over the other knee. "You might consider sticking around Charity City."

"So the legal system can run another con on me?"

Hayden looked amused. "It's not like you had anywhere else to be. You're a retired cop who's between jobs. In spite of your first impression, there are some good people here."

Starting with Jamie, Sam thought. She'd been quite an experience. Sometimes aggravating and frustrating, but certainly never boring. And always invigorating. Especially her kisses. He would never regret knowing her. The thing was, he wouldn't have known her at all if he hadn't been scammed by her family. That's when it dawned on him. He wasn't ticked off about it anymore.

When had that happened?

"Yeah. Good people." Sam stood. "I have to pick

Jamie up before she gets tired of waiting and takes off on her own."

Hayden stood and came around the desk, his gaze assessing. After a moment he said, "You'll get this guy, Sam."

"I hope so. Because if I don't—"

"You will. But if not I'll take care of her for you. Don't worry."

Yeah, like that was going to happen. "I'm counting on you."

Hayden held out his hand and Sam shook it. "It's good to see you, buddy. Jamie's one of the good guys. I hope you'll think about staying."

Sam wished he could *stop* thinking. If Jamie were a guy, there wouldn't be a problem. He wouldn't have kissed her and he wouldn't be concerned about her. Damned annoying that he was worried and it showed. From there it was a hop, skip and jump to caring.

There were so many reasons why that was a bad idea.

Top of the list: he was the wrong man for her.

Chapter Eight

"Sam, will you lighten up?"

"Yeah. I'll do that. When I feel . . . lighter," he said. Situation normal, Sam thought. When he was nervous, he went right to being a smart-ass.

Jamie was sitting behind the desk in her office—against his better judgment. It wasn't the sitting that bothered him. It was that she was in the office at all. She'd insisted on meeting a client, and he'd had no choice but to agree. But as soon as possible, he wanted out of here and back at her place, to get her under wraps—so to speak. That thought led to others making him shift uncomfortably in the chair across from her.

He linked his fingers over his abdomen and shot her

the most intimidating look in his arsenal. "This is a stupid idea."

She tipped her head to the side, taking his measure. "Is that look meant to frighten women and small children? Because, I have to tell you, it's not working. Although I'm not a small child."

He'd noticed. "I don't see why someone else couldn't have handled this," he grumbled.

"She's my client, and it's pro bono. I couldn't ask anyone else."

"Because there's no billable hours."

"Yes," she admitted.

And that, Sam thought, was another problem with her being one of the good guys. She put her money where her mouth was and actually used her power for the powerless.

She met his glare and raised him a scowl. "Are you going to say something? Or are you going to sit there and keep frowning?"

"Yeah."

"You're impossible."

"Thank you." One corner of his mouth quirked up. He leaned forward and rested his elbows on his knees. "The thing is, I don't like you being here."

"But you're here with me. Why is it any different from house arrest?"

"It just is." He held up his hand. "I know. Call it a gut feeling combined with an educated guess. This guy photographed us leaving here, then he got you and your friends right after you left work. This office is the common denominator."

"I see your point, Sam. But I just couldn't blow off this appointment. I'll take full responsibility for the consequences."

"You don't get it," he ground out. "It's not yours to take. It's mine."

"Then I promise not to blame you—"

"I blame me. And there's nothing you can do to change it."

"Sam, what—"

Just then the intercom buzzed and Jamie answered. "Yes?"

"Carol Phelps is here," Peggy said.

"Thanks. Send her in."

"Phelps?" Sam said. "Kevin's mom?"

"Good memory. Yeah, her divorce is almost final."

A woman appeared and knocked lightly on the doorjamb. "Hi."

"Carol, come in."

This tall brunette with sad brown eyes was the psychologically abused woman Jamie had told him about. When she looked at him, her expression turned wary, and he knew that Jamie had been right and divorce was just the first step on her road back.

"This is Sam Brimstone," Jamie explained. "He's my...friend."

Friend? Her eyes wouldn't quite meet his, and the pulse in her throat fluttered like crazy. In a pig's eye they were friends. But he couldn't come up with a better name for what they were and he wasn't about to broadcast that he was her bodyguard. He'd give anything if she didn't need him and hated that she was so vulnerable. He wanted five minutes alone with the creep who was scaring her—no questions asked.

Jamie stood and came around her desk. When the other woman looked surprised at her jeans and yellow, cap-sleeved knit shirt, Jamie explained, "I'm not supposed to be in the office today. I hope you don't mind the way I look."

Carol laughed. "Are you kidding? You could put on orange hair and a clown nose and I'd still think you were a goddess. I can't thank you enough for all your help."

"And it's almost over," Jamie reassured her. She met his gaze. "If you'll excuse us, Sam."

He didn't want to, but she'd play the attorney/client privilege card. "Okay. I'll go annoy the hired help," he said, standing.

Jamie frowned. "Don't give Peggy a hard time."

"I wouldn't dream of it."

He closed the door behind him and went down the hall toward reception. When he passed Al Moore's office, he noted that Slick was still in it. The jerk.

Then he walked over to the reception desk. Peggy looked up and smiled. "She threw you out?"

"Like yesterday's newspaper."

She tapped her long red-painted fingernails on her desk. "Any luck in finding who's been harassing her?"

He shook his head. "I've gone through everything with a fine-tooth comb and found no obvious red flags."

"That stinks." She sighed. "So what happens when your time's up? Can you just walk away?"

"I've got it covered," he said defensively. "She'll be fine."

"It's not her safety I'm talking about. It's her heart."

His own thudded hard. Was she saying what he thought? "I don't—"

"Darn right you don't. For the past few weeks Jamie's had a sparkle in her eyes. A spring in her step. It's like she's finally on the verge of getting a life."

"Good for her."

Peggy wrinkled her nose. "Okay. Play dumb. Isn't it just like a man's brain to shut down about feelings. But just so we're clear, they don't come any better than Jamie. You could—"

Her phone rang, cutting off her assessment of what he could do. Just as well. Every night under Jamie's roof, he tossed and turned in the bed across the hall from hers and ached because of what he couldn't do. She'd told him to lighten up. If he did, he'd be tempted to act on the feelings, and that was the worst thing he could do. He agreed with Peggy that Jamie was the best. But he hoped the receptionist was way off base about the eye sparkles. He didn't want to be anyone's sparkle.

He had about fifteen minutes to brood before Jamie escorted her client to the lobby.

She looked at him. "We're finished."

Carol leaned down to hug her. "Thanks for everything. I don't know what I'd have done without you."

"You're welcome. Say hi to Kevin for me."

"I'll do it." Carol met his gaze. "Nice to meet you, Sam."

"Same here."

Peggy walked around the high reception desk with her purse slung over her shoulder. "It's quitting time. I'll walk out with you," she said to Carol.

Sam kept an eye on the two women exiting through the heavy glass doors, and wondered if the building was being watched. If so, he couldn't tell. Out in the street Carol slid into a small compact car parked at the curb and Peggy made a right turn toward the parking garage with the security guard at her side. Satisfied that both of them were safe, Sam turned back to Jamie. His stomach knotted when he saw her talking to Slick in his office doorway. The jerk's pearly whites would give the Big Bad Wolf some serious competition.

Sam still didn't like the guy, but the reason was clear now. He was jealous as hell.

"So are you going Friday night?" Al asked her.

No one had said anything to him about Friday night. What was the deal? "Going where?" Sam demanded as he walked up beside her.

Jamie's eyes were filled with apology. "It completely slipped my mind, what with everything going on."

"That's understandable," Al said, obviously going

for Dr. Phil's in-touch-with-his-feminine-side award. "But I hope you're not going to let this nutcase win by changing your life and limiting your activities."

Sam could have cheerfully choked him. *Don't make changes even when you're on a wacko's radar* was the sort of dumb remark that came with a high price for anyone who listened.

"What's going on?" he asked again.

"A fund-raiser," she explained. "At the Charity City Country Club."

Sam stared at the other man as he shook his head. "I don't want her out in public."

Al's eyes narrowed and his smile disappeared. "Nothing's going to happen to her with that many people around."

"It's a security nightmare. There's no way to control the situation."

"It's her life and her decision," Al retorted.

"And you're an idiot who knows jack about this," Sam said, barely holding on to his temper. "Thumbing your nose at a nutcase is…nuts."

"So you have a degree in psychology?" Al asked.

His condescending tone made Sam want to deck him. "I'm a cop. I've seen what happens when you don't respect a situation. And you're an arrogant—"

"Excuse me," Jamie interjected, waving her hand. "I'm standing here."

"Sorry." Al smiled, but the edges showed strain. "If you need an escort, I'd be happy to oblige."

"She's not going." Sam's jaw clenched.

"I need to, Sam." The expression in her eyes begged him to understand. "This event raises money for legal aid. It helps people who need legal representation the most and can afford it the least."

Like your mother. She didn't say the words, but the message was clear in her eyes. "Write a check," he said.

"It's not just the money," she retorted. "It's about networking and convincing other attorneys to take on clients who can't pay a standard fee."

She had him and she knew it, Sam realized. If he didn't agree, she'd go anyway. Another bad side to being one of the good guys.

"Okay." He looked at Al and shot him an intimidating look new to his arsenal. "But I'll be the one escorting her."

No way Sam would let her go alone. And he couldn't decide if Slick would be better or worse than letting her solo. The thing was, even though Sam knew he would have to turn her over to someone else soon, he didn't want to do it a second before he had to. And that thought brought zero peace of mind.

What else was new?

Peace of mind had been nonexistent since he'd met Jamie. More specifically, since he'd kissed her. That had been a mistake, and every sleepless night since was the price he paid.

No one knew better than him about mistakes, and he'd be paying for that kiss for the rest of his life.

* * *

"Can you help me with this zipper, Sam?"

Jamie walked into the kitchen, struggling with her dress and didn't see him at first. When she looked up, the view was spectacular. "Wow."

"Wow, yourself." His gaze darkened with something a lot more dangerous than simple appreciation of her little black dress and upswept hair. "If you wore that to court, the jurors would be putty in your hands. The guys, anyway."

"You're exaggerating." So he wouldn't see how much she wanted to believe him, she looked down at the hem of her dress, swirling delicately at her knees. When her emotions were under control, she met his gaze. "But you look amazing."

"Thanks, but I think *you're* exaggerating."

If anything, it was an understatement. He looked amazing in his T-shirt and jeans but the formal look was off the chart. Yesterday they'd shopped so he could buy something appropriate to wear to the country club. Now that she was experiencing the full effect of his ensemble, *appropriate* wasn't exactly the word she'd choose to describe him. The navy suit and red tie did things to his looks worthy of the warning label Overexposure Could Be Hazardous to Your Heart. But her own ensemble was experiencing mechanical difficulties, and this might be her last chance to enjoy the convenience of a man to zip her up.

She turned her back. "I think it's stuck. Can you give me a hand?"

"Sure."

Was it her imagination, or did his voice sound hoarse? She hoped so. She hoped she wasn't the only one feeling things like attraction and lust. It made no sense, but knowing he was affected, too, would make it easier when he was gone.

He moved behind her and when his warm fingers brushed the bare flesh of her back, her heart stuttered. It wouldn't have been so bad if that were her only reaction, but her breathing was rapid and shallow. There was no way he could miss that. Although she wasn't sure she cared. The warm solidness of Sam felt too good.

"Slippery little sucker," he muttered.

"What?" she said, twisting to look over her shoulder.

"Hold still. I can't get it."

"Do I need to get out the drill and pliers?"

"I wish," he said fervently.

For several moments he fiddled with the back of her dress, long enough for his fingers to set her skin on fire and send liquid heat sizzling through her.

Finally she heard him grunt with satisfaction as the zipper closed and the material came together to shield the sensitive skin of her back from his touch.

"Got it."

She turned around, and the expression on his face put

another hitch in her breathing. Want and need twisted together into a look of dark intensity.

"Thank you, Sam."

And she wasn't talking about his success with her zipper.

"Are you all set?"

"Now that I won't flash the legal contingent, yeah," she said.

"Then I guess we better go." His voice was definitely hoarse.

She grabbed her satin evening purse and threw a black shawl around her bare arms.

Sam looked at her. "Are you sure that will be warm enough? Maybe you could wear something heavier? Like a parka and snowsuit?"

She laughed. "Sorry. No. Wouldn't go with my sexy sling-back pumps."

"Too bad," he said, his tone radiating sincere regret.

The little glow from that remark lasted all the way to the country club. She chattered nonstop about everything and anything she could think of, not caring if she sounded like an idiot. She planned to squeeze every ounce of pleasure out of getting dressed up and having Sam as her escort.

When Al had asked to take her, Sam had shut him down cold. Jamie had given it a lot of thought since then. She'd come to the conclusion that any female in that situation would have enjoyed the same ego spurt she had. When the dust settled, there'd been no point in spoiling the warm feeling by telling Sam she would have turned down her associate's invitation. A girl needed to have some secrets and the thorough way Sam had sifted through her life hadn't left her many.

"Here we are," he said, pulling the Mustang into the lot.

Too bad, she thought. She could have been happy just driving around aimlessly all night. But this dinner was for a good cause, she reminded herself.

Her heels clicked on the asphalt as they walked through the parking lot, and his large hand at the small of her back made her feel warm and safe. They stopped at the registration area, then went inside. The main room had a two-story-high ceiling with several crystal chandeliers, suitably dimmed. Round tables filled the area and were covered with white linen cloths and colorful flower arrangements.

Volunteers selling raffle tickets circulated and hit them up as soon as they walked in the door. Jamie and Sam both bought an impressive amount.

She looked up at him. "You didn't have to do that. The per-plate charge is pretty pricey and will net quite a bit for the cause."

"I figured. But like you said, this is important."

"Maybe you'll win something," she said. "Items have been donated by local businesses, and you could wind up with dinner for two at The Homestead."

"That would be lucky." His mouth curved up at the corners. "Although I have connections there."

The thought made her hot all over. "Let's go get a drink," she said, indicating the bar in the corner.

He nodded and after making their way over, Sam

bought a glass of white wine for her and soda water with lime for himself. After taking a sip, he said, "Remember, stay close to me."

Twist my arm, she thought, breathing in the scent of him that was more intoxicating than her Chardonnay. "You don't really think he'd try anything here, do you?"

"Let me put it this way—anyone but your folks or me is a suspect."

"Okay."

She played good little soldier to hide the fact that his words shook her up. She'd allowed herself to forget why he was really there and not even the wine could take the edge off of her twinge of unease.

"I need to mingle," she told him. "It's important to network with business people from the community."

"Understood."

But he wasn't happy, she realized, as they worked their way through the crush of bodies to meet and greet familiar faces. Sam's face grew grimmer by the minute as she shook hands. Finally she spotted Hayden Blackthorn who happened to be standing by himself.

He smiled when he recognized them. "Jamie. Sam. Nice to see you."

Sam shook his hand. "You, too."

Hayden was looking dark and dangerous in his black suit and gray shirt with the pewter-colored tie. Sandwiched between two good-looking men was no reason to complain, and Jamie wasn't about to.

"How's your family?" she asked.

"Fine. And your folks?"

"Good," she answered automatically. But she realized she hadn't had much contact with them since Sam had invaded her life. Clearly they trusted him to take care of her. "They've been keeping a low profile since the auction."

Hayden looked thoughtful. "How much longer will you be in town, Sam?"

Translation—when is your community service complete?

"Six days and counting," Sam answered.

"Okay. Let me know when you want to finalize those arrangements we talked about the other day."

"Will do."

Hayden glanced across the room. "There's someone I need to talk to. Nice seeing you both."

Jamie watched his broad back until the crowd swallowed him. "What was he talking about? What arrangements are you making?"

"It's no big deal," Sam said.

"It's about me, isn't it?" She wasn't sure how she knew. Maybe the way he wouldn't quite look her in the eye.

He studied her for several moments before finally nodding. "I talked to him the day you were ordering the security system."

"About?" she demanded.

"Taking over for me." He ran his fingers through his hair. "You'll be okay with him."

"Isn't that my decision?" She'd already decided to

contact Blackthorn Investigations and wasn't sure why this pushed her buttons. Maybe because it felt like he was anxious to be gone. "In six days and counting, I'm not your problem, Sam. You don't need to take care of anything. And, by the way, when were you going to discuss this with me?"

"Before I left."

Thanks for the reminder, she thought. So much for her fun evening. The irony was that ever since Stu, she'd been wary of men because they said one thing and did just the opposite. But Sam had done exactly what he promised, which meant he would finish his community service and leave Charity City. Something shifted inside her and a door she'd thought closed widened just a crack. Just enough to give her a preview of the pain in store for her when he was gone.

She turned away and started across the room but didn't get far. Sam gripped her arm and tugged her into a secluded corner.

"What?" he demanded.

Her eyes ached with tears she held back. "You can hardly wait to turn me over to someone else."

"You're wrong. It's about the right man to protect you."

"And you're not right? Excuse me, but I think you've done a fine job." When he took a step toward her, she backed up and felt the wall. "I'm still here—walking, talking and ticked off at you."

"What I've done," he ground out, "is lose my objectivity."

She shook her head. "I'm not following."

"That makes two of us. All I know for sure is that I hate being out in public with you. But I can't tell if it's because of the threat to your safety, or the way every man in this room is looking at you." He braced his hands on the wall and hemmed her in, his big body sheltering her, giving them privacy. His eyes were hot, intense as his gaze raked over her. "The thing is, I can't even blame them. The way you look in that dress, I can't imagine any man not wanting you. It's like satin and sin."

Her heart hammered and she could hardly breathe. "Oh, Sam—"

"And I'm no different from every other man here, which means I'm the wrong man to take care of you."

"I don't agree."

"You would if you knew what I'd done—" He shook his head, his expression darkly intense.

"Tell me, Sam. What—"

She felt her cell phone vibrate in her purse. What bad timing! Hoping to be able to ignore it, she checked the Caller ID and saw her mother's number.

She flipped it open. "Mom, hi. I can't talk now—"

"Neither can I." Her mother's voice was tense and strained with a note of panic, too.

Something was wrong. "What is it, Mom?"

"Your father. I think he's having a heart attack. We're at the emergency room."

Chapter Nine

"What's taking so long?"

Jamie's high-heeled pumps clicked on the tile floor of the E.R. as she paced over to the double doors separating the waiting room from the trauma area. God, her feet hurt. If she'd known this was going to happen, she'd have worn comfortable pacing shoes. Emotion clogged her throat and she swallowed hard.

"Your mom said they're doing tests. These things take time," Sam said.

Jamie whirled and stomped back to where he was sitting on a gray-blue chair with shiny metal arms. He'd loosened his tie and tossed his suit jacket on the chair beside him. The long sleeves of his dress shirt were rolled to just below his elbows. It was a supersexy look, and the fact that she could notice at a time like this bothered her on too many levels to count.

Glaring down at him, she said, "Don't patronize me. And for God's sake, don't be reasonable. I can't stand that. I swear if someone doesn't tell me something soon, I'm going to sue this hospital for intentional infliction of emotional distress."

"No, you're not." The corners of his mouth curved up.

"There you go being reasonable again. *And* you're treating me like a child."

"You are." His gaze lowered slightly, and something hot flared in his eyes, then disappeared. "You're a grown-up child whose father could be in trouble."

She flopped in the chair beside him. "This is all my fault."

"How do you figure?" He stretched his arm out along the back of her chair, his long fingers resting dangerously close to her bare shoulder.

She shivered, then met his gaze. "I'm always so stubborn."

"You'll get no argument from me."

"Funny." She huffed out a breath. "I fight him every step of the way. If I'd just listened and tried to compromise— If I didn't always give him reason to worry."

"Here's breaking news, counselor. You don't have the market cornered on blame and guilt." His tone was filled with self-incrimination.

Jamie didn't miss the shadows in his eyes and made

a decision. It was time for him to open up. "What do you blame yourself for, Sam?"

"So many things, so little time." He was trying to dodge the question.

Not again, she thought. "I need you to tell me. You've hinted and danced around it. You've learned, probably the hard way, to respect every situation and not underestimate any threat. I want to know your story partly because I just want to. But mostly because you need to tell someone."

"You're wrong. The last thing I want to do is talk."

"Speaking of wrong, you said I'd understand why you're the wrong man if I knew what you'd done. So tell me."

"Do you remember everything I say?" he asked grimly.

"Pretty much," she agreed.

He glanced toward the double doors. "This isn't the time to talk about it."

She angled her knees toward him. "Don't do that, Sam. My father might be dying. I need something to take my mind off that. I need you to help me understand you. And this is as good a time as any."

He met her gaze and sighed. "Okay. You win." Then he rested his elbows on his knees, linked his fingers together and clammed up.

He'd agreed to talk, but that didn't mean he would give it up easily. Asking questions was what she did best. "Why did you leave LAPD?"

"I'm responsible for a woman's murder."

Jamie was shocked speechless, partly because she

hadn't expected him to be so direct, but mostly because of what he'd said. A woman's murder? She let out a long breath as her mind raced.

"There's more to it than that." There had to be.

The look he slid her was harsh. "She was my best friend's sister."

"What happened?" She carefully filtered from her tone the shock coursing through her.

"I was cocky and arrogant and thought the situation was mine to control."

"Tell me," she encouraged.

He scrubbed his hands over his face, then stared straight ahead, as if he were watching the events of the past unfold in a slide show. "Dave and I went to high school together and hung out all the time. Marcie—his little sister—always tagged along wherever we went. She was like the little sister I never had. We both watched out for her, tried to protect her, screened her dates."

"I bet she hated that," Jamie said, knowing how she must have felt from personal experience.

"She did." He laughed, but there was no warmth in the sound. "Ironically, Dave and I both liked the guy she married."

Jamie willed herself to patience. He needed to tell this in his own way. "But?" she prompted.

"After a couple years she'd turn up with bruises on her arm. A split lip. Black eye she claimed was from being clumsy, running into a door. She wore sunglasses and lots of makeup to hide marks."

"You're right. But I didn't respect the situation. There were things I could have done. Precautions she could have taken. But she said he would win if she had to live in a cage."

Jamie remembered how he'd gone off on Al for saying something similar. "Hindsight is twenty-twenty."

"Yeah." He tugged her close to his chest and wrapped his arms more tightly around her. "That's the story. That's why I left LAPD. A cop who fails to protect and serve has no business staying a cop."

She put her arms around his neck and linked her fingers. After Stu, she'd thought men were genetically predisposed to be weasels. Then along came Sam. Wasn't it just her luck to meet the only guy on the planet who took his promises so much to heart that he walked away from his career when he couldn't keep his word?

Off the top of her head she could count two problems created by his fine-tuned sense of integrity. One, Sam hadn't promised to stay in town. Two, she'd promised never to follow a man again. So it wouldn't be especially smart to break that promise for a man who would be relieved to unload her along with his responsibility for her safety.

But he was still here right now, this moment, with his arms securely around her. She snuggled closer to him even as something pulled tight in her chest. The E.R. was definitely the right place for her, because her father wasn't the only one whose heart hurt.

* * *

"Thank goodness Daddy's going to be okay." Thank goodness she and Sam had finally left the hospital and were on the way home.

The dash lights illuminated Sam's features when he glanced at her. "Yeah. Maybe the false alarm will scare him straight."

Her look was wry. "You mean, into not worrying about me."

"I think he needs to start small, with something he can control. Like improving his diet," Sam said.

"Speaking of diets, can we talk about what you said tonight?"

Since neither of those two things were related, she'd been going for light, but obviously failed. The silence echoing through the small car was a big clue.

"Sam?"

Every single streetlight they passed illuminated the grim expression on his face. "I'm sorry I told you. There's nothing left to say. Like everyone else, you think that I should just get over it."

"Everyone?"

"I saw the department shrink for a while."

"Oh."

And it hadn't helped, Jamie realized. Because he still blamed himself. There was nothing more she could say. But that poor woman's tragic death wasn't what she'd meant.

"Did you mean what you said at the country club?"

"About hiring Hayden?" He glanced at her, then returned his gaze to the road. "Yeah."

Jamie sighed as she shook her head in exasperation. She was going to choke the man with her bare hands—assuming she could get them around his thick, strong neck.

"Leave it to a man to avoid the personal," she muttered. "I was talking about what you were about to say just before my mother called, that you were the wrong man to take care of me if I knew what you'd done…"

It sounded like he groaned, but road noise made it hard to tell. "Leave it to a woman to never forget anything a man says."

"Not a chance."

"How I wish you would. Just this once."

"By now you should know avoiding an issue isn't my style."

"People can change."

"Yes," she said. "They make mistakes and face up to them. Try to make up for what they've done."

His gaze was guarded when he glanced at her. "Why do I get the feeling that suddenly we're not talking about me?"

"Because we're not." She'd get to him in a minute. But something else was on her mind. "I've been thinking about your father."

"Why?"

"Because I faced losing my father tonight and it was pretty horrible. But if we had a gazillion unresolved issues between us, it would compound the devastation."

"Not for me," he snapped. "I hated what he did to my mother."

"And rightly so. But you never said you hated him."

"Your point?" The edge to his voice could cut glass.

"You're nothing like him, Sam."

"I'm not sure where you're going with this, Counselor."

"You became a cop—not a lawyer like him—to help people on a grass-roots level. A first responder. You won't touch the money he left you that could, and should, have gone to your mother."

"He turned his back on us. Then at the end he was alone and tried to buy me back. That's all it was about. Not that he'd changed."

"Maybe. And that's my point. He's gone and you'll never know what was in his heart."

"It doesn't matter."

"You're wrong. If it didn't, you'd take the money he left and do something good with it." She put her hand on his arm. "It's okay for you to care, Sam. You'd never let down someone you love. You're not like him."

"Right."

Jamie felt the tension running through him and knew she'd struck a nerve. She also knew she'd said as much as she could, gone as far as possible, and he didn't want to talk about it anymore.

So it was time for the other thing on her mind. "So now can we talk about the fact that you want me?"

This time his groan came through loud and clear

because he'd stopped the car in front of her house. In the driver's seat, he half turned toward her. Was there anything sexier on the planet than a man with his sleeves rolled up and his tie loosened? Her gaze strayed to the muscles rippling in his forearm and his long fingers with their white-knuckled grip on the steering wheel.

"I didn't mean that the way it sounded," he said

But the look in his eyes said something different. "So how *did* you mean it?" she asked.

"I was trying to make a point."

"And I got it," she agreed. But she wasn't sure the message she got wasn't simply something she wanted to hear and not at all what he'd meant.

There was no time like the present to sort it out. Because soon she would have no time at all.

"So was it just the dress? Or me in—"

"There's someone in the house." There was no emotion in the tensely spoken words. He was all business.

"What?" Her heart jumped as she looked out the passenger window. They'd left the porch light on and the interior illuminated. The lace curtains in the living room hid nothing. "I don't see anything."

"A shadow moved in the hall." He reached across her knees and opened the glove compartment, then pulled out a large, heavy-looking, squarish pistol.

"What are you going to do?"

"I'm finally gonna take this guy down."

Everything in her cried out against him going in there alone. "Wouldn't it be better to call the sheriff?"

"He'll get away." He pulled off his tie, then slipped the ammunition clip from his gun to check it before slapping it into the grip. Then his gaze locked with hers. "Stay here."

"Being your basic coward and not the plucky but dim-witted heroine of a bad B movie, I plan to." When one corner of his mouth quirked up, she said, "What?"

"Never just say 'okay' when you can use twenty-five words instead." Before she could think of a come-back, he cupped her cheek in his hand. "You'll be fine."

"I know."

"Lock the doors and call the sheriff on your cell."

"Okay." She put her small hand over his larger one and met his gaze. "I can't talk you out of this?"

"Not a chance."

"I was afraid of that."

He took her hand and dropped a quick kiss in her palm. "You'll be okay," he said again.

"Not a doubt in my mind," she said firmly. "I trust you with my life. Completely."

"Good to know." He had the audacity to grin. "All the same, lock these doors and keep your head down."

"Okay." Before he could close the driver's door, she said, "Sam?"

He leaned down and met her gaze. "Yeah?"

"Be careful."

"Always. Now lock these doors. Call the sheriff."

"I'm on it," she said, pulling her phone from her satin evening bag. First she locked the doors, then made the

911 call and was told it would be at least fifteen minutes before a patrol car could get there.

For the first time, Jamie realized the downside of living so far from Charity City proper. She was grateful to have Sam, and at the same time she was terrified something would happen to him. Already tonight she'd faced the very real possibility of losing someone she loved. Her feelings about Sam were dangerously close, and she wondered if she was in love with him.

She hoped not. More than that, she hoped he would come back and tell her it was another false alarm.

It seemed like forever and she couldn't imagine what was taking so long. Her house wasn't that big. Just when she thought she'd lose her mind, the front door opened wide and Sam appeared with someone. He had the guy's arm bent up behind his back and was nudging him forward. It was a young man, she realized. They stopped under the porch light, and she recognized Kevin Phelps.

She unlocked her door and got out of the car, then slowly walked up the steps. "What's going on?"

"I didn't mean any harm." Kevin looked scared.

Sam kept a firm grip on the gangly teen as he met her gaze. His expression was grim. "Someone has a crush on you."

Chapter Ten

The next day Sam escorted Jamie from the sheriff's station still feeling uneasy. They'd given their statements to the law-enforcement types, and the county prosecutor was mulling over the charges to file in court. But something was bothering him, and he couldn't put his finger on it.

He stopped her on the sidewalk, under the awning just outside the heavy double doors. "You are going to press charges, right?"

Jamie met his gaze. "I haven't made up my mind."

And yet again she was leading with that soft heart of hers. That quality was what had made him ask in the first place. It made him want to shake her at the same time he fought the urge to pull her into his arms and protect her.

He wanted her and was still kicking himself for saying it out loud. He wanted her—in that country-club outfit that made her look like sin and satin or in the jeans and cropped T-shirt that she wore now. The little top molded to her breasts and moved with her, giving him forbidden glimpses of the soft, smooth skin of her abdomen.

The late-spring day was warm, but that wasn't why he was sizzling through and through. It could snow in Dallas in July and he'd still be hot for the curvy counselor and her soft marshmallow heart. But more than anything, he wanted her safe.

"What's stopping you?" he asked, about pressing charges.

"A lot of things." She folded her arms over her chest. "For one thing, he didn't hurt me."

"I guess not. If you like being followed, scared and forced to hunker down in your house."

She looked troubled. "I still can't believe Kevin would do this."

Sam felt the same way, but decided to play devil's advocate. "Don't go soft, Jamie. He broke into your house."

"But he was leaving me a rose—"

"On your pillow."

"Because he saw my father taken to the E.R. by paramedics and knew I'd be upset."

"He's been to your house before," Sam pointed out.

"With pictures of girls' night out."

"Which he followed you to get. Sheriff's detectives

checked it out and he wasn't working at the restaurant that night."

"But there was no harm done," she insisted.

"He unscrewed the porch lightbulb, and that's deliberate psychological battery." Sam frowned as he voiced his thoughts. "Then there was the picture they found in his wallet."

"The one of me taken from my dad's desk," she said.

"He had access to your e-mail through your parents' computers at work. And these days a six-year-old is savvy enough to send digital pictures over the Internet."

"It doesn't look good, does it?"

"The circumstantial evidence is pretty convincing." So why was he uneasy about it? Sam wondered.

"I just don't know about pressing charges," she insisted. "He's a mixed-up teenager caught between his parents in a bitter divorce."

"And he fixated on the beautiful attorney—"

"Hold it." Her face brightened for a moment. "You think I'm beautiful?"

Hell, yes, he thought. But he'd done enough damage with his big mouth. "I'm role playing. This is Kevin we're talking about. He's got more testosterone than common sense. And his mom's divorce lawyer got him out of trouble."

"And cut him a break with a job," Jamie finished. "You said it last night. He's got a crush. There's no law against that."

"No. But most teenage boys pass notes in study hall or get a friend to run interference."

"I'm not in high school," she pointed out.

Yeah. He'd noticed. "I'm just saying his behavior isn't normal."

"Like I said—he's mixed up. He needs counseling, not incarceration."

"Some time in a juvenile facility would do both."

"But at what cost? Those places are full of pretty hardened offenders—even if they are juveniles. A sensitive boy like Kevin could be exposed to worse things on his road to rehabilitation."

Especially if it hadn't been Kevin who'd done all those things, Sam thought. But he kept it to himself because he didn't want to scare her unnecessarily.

"I guess we're at an impasse," he said. Not unlike the first time they'd met in her office.

"Yeah." She frowned. "I guess I don't need a bodyguard any longer."

And that shook him like a blast from a concussion grenade. He hadn't thought about that. She didn't need him any longer. The realization made him feel hollow inside, empty. The idea of leaving Jamie was about as appealing as walking naked in a hail storm. That very first day he'd told her something had to give. He'd had no idea it would be the safe zone around his heart.

"I still have a couple more days of community service left," he reminded her.

She slid her hands into the pockets of her jeans. "Now that I'm safe, you know Uncle Harry wouldn't care."

But I would, he thought. He just wasn't ready to say goodbye yet. "I'm not sure Uncle Harry would look kindly on shaving days off a mandated sentence."

"I could talk to him—"

"You trying to get rid of me?"

Something flared in her eyes, and he couldn't tell if he'd hit a bull's-eye or was way off the mark. But he wouldn't ask. Knowing for sure wouldn't change anything.

"You don't have to answer that, Counselor." Sam curved a finger beneath her chin and nudged her gaze up to his. "How about I take you to lunch at The Homestead and we can give your parents the news?"

"News?" Hayden Blackthorn came up behind him. "Hi, you two. You're looking pretty serious about something."

Sam hadn't heard him approach. He'd been too preoccupied with Jamie. He shook hands with the other man. "Hayden."

"Sam caught the guy who's been harassing me." Jamie angled her head toward the double smoked-glass doors of the sheriff's department. "We just gave our statements. I'm on my way to give my parents the good news."

"I'm sure they'll be relieved," Hayden said.

"You go on ahead," Sam told her.

She nodded. "This can't wait. After that health scare with my dad, I want to eliminate any possible stress."

"I'll meet you there."

She nodded. "Bye, Hayden."

Sam watched the sexy swing of her hips as she walked down the street. He memorized every line, curve and sway because in a matter of days, memories would have to be enough.

"Too bad you're not sticking around."

Sam didn't miss the amusement in the other man's gaze. "I am. For another couple of days."

"Okay. So what did you want to talk to me about?"

So, Hayden got it. Sam was glad Jamie had been too preoccupied with telling her parents the breaking news, or a smart cookie like her would have challenged him about why he was sending her on ahead. What he had to say to Hayden, he didn't want her to hear.

Sam filled the other man in on everything that had happened since they'd seen him at the country club. Less than twenty-four hours ago, he realized. It seemed like years, yet he hadn't had time to think about why he'd told Jamie about his reason for leaving LAPD. Or how he felt about her knowing.

"The thing is," Sam said, "I have my doubts that Kevin is responsible for everything that happened."

"Why?" Hayden folded his arms over his chest.

"He's not a hardened criminal, just a regular kid."

His friend's expression was grim. "There are stories in the news every day about stuff nobody thought a regular kid would do."

He had a point. "What bothers me is that his story hasn't changed, even with experienced investigators questioning him. He copped to B&E to leave the rose and taking her photo, but flatly denies everything else."

"So what are you saying?"

"I'm not sure." Sam rubbed his palm across the back of his neck. "It's just my detective's sixth sense telling me that something's off."

"I've known you a long time, Sam. I'd take your sixth sense over the next guy's hard evidence anytime."

"That means a lot to me." But Sam had good reason to doubt his expertise. And local law enforcement was convinced the danger was over. "Then maybe you won't mind doing me a favor."

"Name it."

"Watch over Jamie for me. When I'm gone. Unofficially."

"You know I will," Hayden agreed. "But you could stay and keep an eye on her yourself. Blackthorn Investigations could use someone like you. Your experience and expertise. I'd like to have that sixth sense of yours on my payroll."

Sam smiled. "No, thanks. Although I'm flattered."

And tempted. For so many reasons, all of them leading back to Jamie. But she was also the reason he couldn't stay.

He didn't want her to count on him.

In spite of what she believed, there was too much of his father in him, and sooner or later he'd let her down. She'd been hurt enough to last a lifetime by a guy who'd sweet-talked her, then walked away. From the beginning she'd known he was going, and he'd thought it would be easy to leave. He couldn't have been more wrong. Wherever he was, whatever he was doing, he would always think about her and wonder if she was safe. Because he cared about her. Which was why he intended to stick to the plan. Get out of her life after thirty days of bodyguard duty.

Unfortunately, while he'd been guarding her body, he'd forgotten to guard his heart.

The night of Sam's farewell dinner, Jamie looked around the table. Her parents had insisted on throwing the party at The Homestead to celebrate the end of his community service and a successful outcome of their auction purchase.

Uncle Harry was there, sitting at the head of the oblong table. Next to him on either side, her parents faced each other. They'd turned the restaurant operation over to a manager while this dinner was going on in a back room. Hayden Blackthorn and his widowed mother sat facing each other on either side of her parents. They'd been delighted to be asked. His daughter, Emily, was at a slumber party and he'd said a grown-up get-together would be a real treat in spite of the fact it was about saying goodbye. Then there was Sam and her, facing each other. She thought *celebration* and *saying goodbye* had to be darn close to an oxymoron.

Her heart cracked a little more, and she prayed Sam wouldn't see. It's not like she hadn't known this was coming. He'd never promised to stay. In spite of what he thought, he was a man who kept his promises.

She couldn't keep wallowing. She needed to be proactive in this party.

She stood, and everyone ignored her, so she tapped her wineglass with a spoon. When she had their attention, she said, "I propose a toast. To Sam Brimstone, the best bodyguard a girl ever had."

Murmurs of agreement buzzed around the table, and everyone lifted their glasses. "To Sam."

He sipped from his long-necked bottle of beer, and amusement glittered in his eyes as he looked at her. "You're singing a different tune, Counselor. Thirty days ago you tried to throw me out of your office."

"Not literally. Bouncer isn't in my job description." Just as she'd done then, her gaze dropped to his broad shoulders and wide chest. If she sighed, she figured no one heard. The hum of voices in the room would cover her.

"But you were not a happy camper," he recalled.

Her eyes widened in mock outrage. "Oh? And you were doing the dance of joy at the prospect of thirty days fluff patrol?"

"Fluff patrol?" One dark eyebrow rose as he set his beer on the white linen tablecloth. "I believe of the two of us, I was the one who actually took the situation more seriously."

"I just didn't want to believe it. Kevin…" She shook her head.

Something flitted across his face, and it wasn't satisfaction for a job well done. She figured he was as con-flicted about the teenager as she. Kevin Phelps was in a juvenile facility, and Jamie planned to visit him soon.

At the other end of the table, Uncle Harry stood. He didn't have to tap a glass to get everyone's attention. Maybe it was the judge thing, Jamie thought.

"I'd like to propose a toast. To Samuel Owen Brim-stone."

This was the first time she'd heard his middle name. Their gazes locked and she mouthed, "SOB?"

One corner of his mouth quirked up when he shrugged.

"Sam was in my courtroom for assault and battery. While my official stand on violence is that it's not tol-erated for any reason, I feel pretty certain Bo Taggart had it coming."

Sam leaned forward and whispered, "That's what *I* told him."

This time Jamie shrugged.

The judge continued, "You could say I stretched the letter of the law that day. But I've seen a lot of folks in my courtroom and I've come to be a halfway decent judge of character. I can tell when a man's lost. All things considered, I figured it wouldn't do Sam any harm to cool his jets in Charity City for a bit." His gaze met Sam's. "Didn't do my niece any harm, either. Thanks, son, for taking good care of her."

Sam nodded and raised his beer.

Jamie sipped from her wine, then set it on the table and stared at Sam. "So you're not mad at him anymore?"

"Haven't been for a long time."

That was good, she thought. At least when Sam left, he wouldn't be angry. Maybe he'd even have a good memory or two. Like kiss number one, and kiss number two. And he was such a man of his word he hadn't kissed her again. After Stu, she'd never thought she would wish for a man to break his word to her, but they were very good kisses. And now he wasn't responsible for her any longer and would leave right after this dinner was over. When she said goodbye, she planned to show him exactly what he was walking away from.

Hayden Blackthorn stood and everyone grew quiet. Apparently it wasn't a judge thing, just a man thing. He lifted his beer. "Sam Brimstone, a good man, a good friend. And the best detective I've ever worked with. If you change your mind about that job I offered you, you know where to find me."

Jamie's eyes snapped to Sam. He'd had a job offer? He never told her. But why should he? He'd turned it down. Maybe someone should point out to him that changing your mind isn't a bad thing. Women do it all the time. It's different from breaking a promise.

Pain rolled through her in waves. She was hurting for him and what he wouldn't accept and also for herself because the two of them would never have a chance to find out what could have been.

What a colossal waste. Some people spent their whole lives searching for that one and only special someone who made their heart beat faster, that single person to put faith and trust in. They'd stumbled across each other through sheer luck, and he was going to spit in Fate's eye.

She wasn't a male basher, but maybe there was some truth in them being obtuse and pig-headed.

Her father stood and everyone around the table grew quiet again. Definitely a guy thing. "To Sam," he said. "A man of extraordinary courage and integrity. Thank you from the bottom of my heart. And it's healthy, so I'm told." He held up his wineglass. "This is a fine Cabernet, for heart health."

Uncle Harry held up his own red wine. "For medicinal purposes. To Sam."

Everyone clinked glasses as Jamie remembered that night in the E.R. Her mother had been with her father and Sam was with her. She'd been so grateful for his support. The personal details he'd shared had been above and beyond the call of bodyguard duty. She held out a tiny hope that he cared about her just a little. And maybe the telling of his story had helped him as much as hearing it had helped her that night.

Last but not least, her mother stood, and the voices stopped again.

"Thank you, Sam," Louise said. "I wish there were words to adequately convey my gratitude for taking care of my only daughter. The best I can come up with is—I think you should take Hayden up on his offer and stay here with us in Charity City."

Jamie's eyes burned with tears and she struggled not

to let them fall. Sam squirmed when everyone clapped, cheered and tapped their glasses. To anyone who didn't know, it simply looked like modesty. But Jamie knew he couldn't forgive himself and he'd lost his soul. If he couldn't find it here in Charity City, he wouldn't be able to find it anywhere.

The thought of that sliced clear through her—not for herself. For him. She couldn't stand the idea of him so lost. It was a measure of how much she cared. It was the reason she—

Loved him?

Was she in love with him? Was it possible all the warning bells had made no difference?

Just then an ear-splitting siren blared through the restaurant. She'd never heard it before, but knew it was the fire alarm. Her heart started to pound and the beginning of panic made her look around frantically to see what everyone else was doing.

Then Sam was there, coolly taking her arm, leading her out the back door. The weird thing was, she didn't smell smoke or see a hint of anything wrong.

Chapter Eleven

"After all that excitement at the restaurant, it's a good thing my father got a clean bill of health."

Sam glanced up, then put his shaving kit in his duffel bag along with the clothes he'd just packed. "Has he ever mentioned a problem like that before?"

"You mean a false alarm with the fire alarm?"

"Yeah."

Jamie was desperately trying to keep the mood light, but his serious expression made it even harder. If she couldn't take cover in humor, his last memory of her would be a blubbering mess.

"He never said anything to me. But I'll feel better after his electrician checks out all the wiring. I'm sure it's nothing."

"Make sure he follows through with that."

"I will."

He zipped the bag, and she winced at the mournful sound. This was really goodbye. It was just wrong, she thought.

"Looks like I got everything." He glanced around the room, then hefted the bag onto his shoulder and headed for the front door. "Helps to travel light."

That helped nothing, but she wouldn't beg him to stay. "Sam, you don't have to go." That wasn't actually begging, right?

He set his bag by the door. "It's time. My thirty days are up, and I'm not your bodyguard now."

"Now you're my friend." He was so much more, but that's not what he wanted to hear. "Stay the night and get an early start in the morning."

His eyes caught fire before he banked the glow. "You know why I can't."

"I know what you told me, but that doesn't mean I should stop trying to convince you you're a good man. Hayden said you're the best detective he's ever worked with."

"You're good, Counselor. But even for you, convincing me would be an uphill battle."

This was about the woman he couldn't save. "Sam, listen to me." She prayed to the god of glib to give her the right words to convince this incredibly good and decent man that he wasn't to blame. "You're not responsible for the actions of an unbalanced man obsessed with evil."

"It's not that simple."

"I know. Being a cop is complicated, difficult, thankless. You see all the bad stuff."

"That's an understatement."

"I know," she said again. "I've seen it, too. Not like you have, but lawyers are the next line of defense. We get temporary restraining orders and work with the police to protect victims. It's not always enough. When a relationship is beyond repair, we end it legally. The worst is seeing what happens to the kids caught up in the middle."

"Yeah. It can get pretty ugly."

"No one knows that better than you. And you're only human—flesh and blood like the rest of us. And flawed— just like the rest of us."

"Cops are held to a higher standard," he argued.

"And your personal standards are higher yet. But you can't stop trying to make a difference."

"That's the thing. *I* can't make a difference anymore."

"That's not true. You're not perfect and no one expects you to be. All anyone expects is your best."

He ran his fingers through his hair as he huffed out a breath. "You're right. I've had to deal with a lot of bad people. And I did my best."

"I believe you. The man I've come to know wouldn't do less."

"But, Jamie, I let down the people I *care* about. And not just once. I couldn't help my mother. And I cost Marcie her life. There are flaws, but mine are *flaws* with a capital *F*. I have to live with it. But I just couldn't live with myself if I let you down, too."

"You'd never do that. And you can't lose hope." She put her hand on his arm, needing to be connected on the outside as she tried to reach what was wrong inside. "Here's the thing, Sam, you can't stop trying. For every person you can't save, there's one you can."

One corner of his mouth quirked up. "Like I said, you're good, Counselor. But—"

"No buts. You've got to stop running sometime, Sam."

"Why?"

"Because all the baggage comes with you, no matter how light you travel."

He shook his head. "Don't you ever get tired?"

"Of what?"

"Trying."

"Not when there's something worth trying for," she answered.

"Then you need to save it for someone who matters. I'm a lost cause."

"Don't say that—" The knot of emotion spreading from her heart slid into her throat, choking off her words.

Earlier she'd resolved to show him what he was walking away from when he said goodbye. Now would be a good time, if she could hold back the tears and save them for when she was alone.

"Jamie." Her name was hardly more than a breath on his lips as he pulled her into his arms.

She let him hold her because she was too spineless

to give him up just yet. She savored the closeness and warmth, the pounding of his heart against her cheek. Maybe this was a sign that she'd gotten through to him.

"You don't have to go tonight, Sam," she said again.

He kissed her hair, then set her away from him. "Yeah. I do. Or I'd make a big mistake, and you don't need that when you get on with your life."

The hope that had burned so brightly just a moment ago sputtered and dimmed. "What if I said I don't want to?"

"Then you'd be lying. I know you want a family. Settle down. Get married. Have babies with your husband. Charity City must be full of nice guys. You need to find a man."

"I found one," she retorted.

"You're relentless."

"You have no idea." She took a step forward and they were toe-to-toe. Looking up, meeting his gaze and putting all the feelings pouring through her into her own eyes, she said, "You only ever broke one promise to me."

"One is enough," he said grimly.

"No. It wasn't nearly enough. And, frankly, I didn't mind at all."

"I don't—"

"You said kissing me while I was under your protection was unprofessional, and as long as you were on the court's time, it wouldn't happen again."

"I made a mistake—"

"See, that's the thing. It didn't feel like a mistake to me. There's that whole holding-yourself-to-a-higher-standard thing again. But your community service is over. You're not here in a professional capacity now."

"Which is why I need to walk away while I still can."

"About walking away—" She leaned into him and slid her arms around his neck. "Far be it from me to lead you into temptation, but I promised myself that I'd show you exactly what you're walking away from."

Conflict raged in his eyes, and his body tensed for a moment. Then she felt his surrender.

"Ah, hell," he muttered.

He lowered his head and crushed her mouth with his. She tasted want, need and desperation on his lips. He kissed her eyes, nose, cheeks and chin, then moved on to a very responsive little spot on her neck, directly below her ear. She shivered, and a small moan escaped her lips as she tipped her head to the side, giving him better access. She could hear his ragged breathing and had enough sanity left to be grateful that she wasn't the only one having difficulty drawing in air. Then he moved back to her mouth, kissing her until she thought he'd swallow her whole.

She felt his reluctance when he pulled away and drew in a deep breath. "So," she said shakily, "I guess I showed you."

"I guess you did," he answered, his voice raspy with passion. His hands shook as he cupped her face in his palms and kissed her softly on the mouth, one last time. His gaze danced over her face as if he were committing her features to memory. "You sure don't make it easy."

"Good."

One corner of his mouth curved up, then he turned away and grabbed his duffel before going out the door. She followed him outside and swore she heard her heart break but probably it was the trunk slamming. He didn't look at her before getting in the car.

With all her might she hung on to his last words and was glad it hadn't been easy for him to walk away.

Standing on the top porch step, she watched until she could no longer see the Mustang's red taillights. Darkness closed in around her along with a deep and profound loneliness. The tears she'd struggled to keep him from seeing spilled over and slid down her cheeks. She was officially a blubbering mess.

Which was why she didn't know someone was waiting in the porch shadows until he grabbed her from behind.

Sam headed for the interstate and got on at the first ramp. He'd planned to find a motel room and get some sleep before resuming his journey to nowhere. But there was a problem with that plan. Thoughts of Jamie wouldn't let him sleep.

Her offer to spend the night with her had been tempting, then her goodbye had nearly shredded his resolve. If he'd once looked at her, either before he got in the car or in the rearview mirror, he wouldn't have been able to leave her.

And leaving her was for her own good. Right?

"Thirty days ago it was right," he mumbled.

Now he wasn't so sure. She was all alone. Or maybe that was the isolation of the pitch-black night and his own loneliness talking. He'd only been gone ten or fifteen minutes and he missed her, everything about her, from the sweet smell of her skin to her sassy mouth that he'd enjoyed kissing speechless.

But not before she'd given him food for thought.

He had to forget about her. Hayden was on the job. But there was no job because the cops closed the case with Kevin's arrest.

"But I've got a bad feeling about that," he said to himself.

The kid never did confess. Then there was the unexplained fire alarm at the restaurant. When no one admitted to pulling it, the incident was chalked up to a wiring problem. Sam wasn't so sure. And with Kevin still in juvie, if anything funny was going on, he couldn't be responsible.

Up ahead the blackness of the road was shattered by the billboard that had started his thirty day detour. Spotlights illuminated the words, Charity City, The Town That Lives Up To Its Name.

At first he hadn't thought so, but a short time with Jamie had changed his mind. And she wasn't the only one. Hayden was there, making a good life for himself and his daughter after the trauma of a bad marriage. Roy and Louise Gibson had trusted him, more important, *entrusted* him with the welfare of their miracle child. They'd treated him like a member of the family. And even Uncle Harry had turned out to be okay. Sam couldn't fault his motivation to protect his niece.

They'd all embraced him and made him feel like one of their own. But it always came back to Jamie.

Her words kept going through his mind. "You can't hold yourself responsible for what an unbalanced man obsessed with evil did."

And that's when his detective radar kicked in big-time. There was still evil out there with Jamie in its crosshairs. He could feel it. And he'd left her when she needed him. Just like the creep in New York. He could feel that, too. But this was one wrong he could change.

He exited the interstate at the next off-ramp, went under the highway and back the way he'd come. Probably he was wrong about the danger. As Jamie had once pointed out, he wasn't a mind reader. Nothing would make him happier than to be wrong. But he was going back, because something was finally right.

He'd found himself; he knew what he wanted. And he thought the fates were probably getting a good belly laugh out of this. Jamie was a lawyer; she deserved someone better. And he wanted her, anyway.

He was in love with her.

And he needed to hear her voice. He pulled his cell phone off the holster on his belt and hit speed dial for her home number.

Jamie wondered who had called. Silly. She had way more to worry about than that. Her biggest problem was the man standing two feet away who'd pointed his big gun and ordered her not to answer the phone. Was hostage fear like stage fright? They said after ten minutes, you relaxed and stopped shaking. By her count it had been fifteen and she was still terrified. But giving a speech and facing down an unbalanced man obsessed with evil were two very different nightmares.

The thought made her think of Sam and wish for the gazillionth time that he were here. He'd know how to disarm this guy. Up till now, all this unbalanced man had done was rant about everything that had gone wrong in his life. She could only hope venting was his primary objective, but then he wouldn't need the gun. Behind him, the front door was ajar—he'd neglected to secure it after wrestling her inside. His back was to the window, and she remembered Sam telling her the lace curtains were no protection from prying eyes.

When she saw headlights coming up the long road, she knew whoever it was must be coming here since there was nothing else around. This might cut her a break, but not if this guy saw and had time to plan. Then someone would just be walking into a trap. She had to keep this guy talking, distract him, disrupt his train of thought.

"So Mr. Phelps—"

The car's lights suddenly disappeared and she wanted to scream. From hopeful to helpless in a heartbeat was the path to panic.

"What?" He stood there with the gun at his side.

She felt as if she were drowning. They said if you panic in the water, you *would* drown. She had to keep her head.

"Kevin looks like his mother."

Why should she find it comforting that the teen looked nothing like the man who'd fathered him? Bill Phelps was tall and muscular. The shaggy hair growing nearly to the collar of his shirt was black, and his brown eyes were cold. She'd always thought Kevin's eyes were like the color of hot cocoa, but there was nothing warm about this man's gaze.

"His loss" was all he said.

She winced, realizing the remark could have set him off. She was walking a fine line and needed to be careful. Although it was far from cold, she shivered. "So, I guess you're the one who's been harassing me."

"Good guess."

"How did you get my e-mail address?"

"From my kid."

"He gave it to you?" she said, surprised.

He shook his head as he rubbed the barrel of the gun on the denim covering his leg. "I took it from the address book on his computer. The one I gave him," he said bitterly. "It's your fault I lost my family."

"How do you figure?"

"You're a lawyer. You made it happen."

"I did the paperwork. That's all."

"If you hadn't done it for free, my wife never would have gone through with the divorce."

"Why do you think she wanted one in the first place?"

"Because she's a stupid bitch. And the kid who looks like her doesn't give me any respect."

"Is that why you let him take the blame for harassing me?" How could a father do something like that?

He shrugged. "He didn't respect me. When you do something wrong, there are consequences. This is his punishment."

Sound parenting strategy spoken in a calm, reasonable voice. Why didn't that reassure her? Because the reasoning was flawed. In his deranged state of mind, anything was wrong if it wasn't what he wanted. And that made it a punishable offense. His wife and son had been living in this hell of control, abuse and fear for so long. Jamie was glad she'd helped them escape it. She'd do it again for anyone who needed her—provided she got out of this alive.

She would. She had to. No way would she let him win.

"So you followed me, too," she said, to keep him talking. The longer he bragged, the more time she had to come up with a way out.

"Yeah. I staked out your office. The rest was easy."

Sam had been right, she thought grimly. She looked at the gun in his hand and shivered at the idea of him watching her. Don't let him see fear. His kind smelled it and fed on it. Reveled in the control it gave him.

"By the way, thanks for the pictures. Your camera takes really good ones. There was one I particularly liked of my friends and me at the Lone Star."

"You're welcome. Too bad your guy showed up. I thought that was my chance when you came alone."

"Sam's a pretty good detective," she agreed, struggling to keep her tone conversational. "His theory was that my office was the common denominator."

"I figured he was the one keeping you out of sight. But that just meant I had to be patient a little longer. Sooner or later you'd have to go back to work or he'd leave town when his time was up. And it's up now."

"You were at the restaurant tonight," she guessed.

He grinned his satisfaction. "Dull party. I thought it could use a little emergency to liven things up." He took a step closer. "Kind of like this party."

Jamie held her ground. "You don't really want to hurt me."

"Yes, I do. You ruined my life. That was wrong. Now it's payback time."

Just then the front door slammed open and Sam barreled inside. Startled, Phelps turned, pointing the gun at the intruder. Jamie's heart pounded, fearing for Sam. She didn't think. Instinct took over and she grabbed the other man's arm, hanging on for all she was worth to throw him off balance.

"Jamie," Sam bellowed. "Get out of the way."

He charged forward and she let go. Before Phelps could lift his arm, Sam grabbed his wrist and yanked it up, so the pistol was pointing at the ceiling. Sam jabbed his elbow into Phelps's stomach and followed up with a knee to the groin. The other man screamed and crumpled to the floor, letting the gun slip out of his hand. Sam kicked it away, then rammed his knee into Phelps's back and pulled his arms behind him while the pinned man groaned in pain.

Breathing hard, Sam looked at her. "Are you all right?"

"Yes."

"Thank God." He closed his eyes for a moment as he let out a long breath, then met her gaze again. "I'll watch him. You go call the sheriff."

Chapter Twelve

Feeling as if she'd been run over by a truck, Jamie stood in the doorway as the deputy put a handcuffed Bill Phelps into the back of a squad car. The lights on top eerily cut the dark night with red and blue slashes of color. Why did the police always take such care that perps didn't hit their heads? Duh, she thought. Some lawyer she was. Liability, of course. It was the best in the world, but what a screwy legal system they had. And Kevin was stuck in it thanks to his father.

"Sheriff?"

The tall man dressed in khaki turned. He was the strong, stalwart, silent type with a sprinkling of gray in the dark hair at his temples. "Yes, ma'am?"

"Will you see to it that Kevin Phelps is released to his mother as soon as possible?"

Politely he touched the brim of his brown uniform hat. "I'll see to it personally, Ms. Gibson."

"Thank you." She started to turn away, then stopped and said, "One last favor. Will you tell him I'll see him soon? We have some things to talk over."

"I'll do it."

She nodded. "Thank you for everything."

"We're just sweepin' up the mess. You're lucky Mr. Brimstone was here."

"Yeah." Lucky and scared.

She closed the door and looked around the now-quiet living room while Sam stood and watched her, arms folded over his chest. Instantly her mind replayed the terror, and she wondered if she'd always see that awful man whenever she entered the room. Would the memory of the violence ever fade? She didn't think she'd ever forget the scene. Sam rushing to her rescue with a pistol pointed at him. The fear that he'd be hurt—or worse.

That's when reaction set in and she started to shake. In two strides, Sam was beside her, then she was in his arms. She burrowed against his warmth and rested her cheek on his chest, listening to the strong, steady beat of his heart. She pressed her face into him when the sobs started. He tightened his hold and murmured meaningless words in a soothing voice. She wasn't sure how long they stood there, but finally she forced herself to get a grip.

She took a step back and pressed the heels of her palms to her eyes, brushing away the lingering moisture. Then she saw the wet spots on the front of Sam's T-shirt. "Sorry about that."

"No harm done. I won't melt."

Since her legs were still shaky, she decided to sit on the sofa. "I don't know why I did that."

"I guess you needed a good cry." The cushion dipped when he sat beside her.

"I remember once," she said, feeling compelled to explain the weakness. "When I was a kid, I got separated from my folks at an amusement park. I walked around through the crowd for an hour and got more and more scared. But I kept it together. Then I saw my mother. When she hugged me, I burst into tears. It was like finally I was with the person who made me feel safe and it was okay to let go."

When a tear rolled down her cheek, he brushed it away with his thumb. "You're safe now, Jamie."

Her mouth trembled when she smiled. "I know. It's all over now. I can't believe it. And thanks to you, I'm okay."

"I'm not."

Her eyes widened and she reached out to touch him. "You're hurt? Where? Why didn't you say something. Do we need to go to the hospital?"

"It's not like that."

"You scared me. Don't ever do that again." She studied his face, the worry lines in his forehead, tension around his mouth, intensity making his blue eyes as bright as the light on the squad car. "How are you not okay?"

"I've faced danger more than once. That goes with the territory when you're a cop." His gaze never left hers, and he looked as if he couldn't look at her hard enough. "But I've never been as scared as I was tonight when I thought he was going to hurt you and I couldn't get to you fast enough."

"That makes two of us."

"But I left you with him." There was self-accusation in his expression.

She shook her head. "You didn't know he was here."

"You deserve better than me." He rested his elbows on his knees and dangled his hands between them. "I tried so hard not to care for you because you deserve better."

She got that he was trying to tell her something important, but her mind was a little slow. Fallout from getting the stuffing scared out of her followed by a world-class crying jag. Still, something stirred inside her that felt suspiciously like hopefulness.

"I never expected to see you again, Sam. I thought you were on the road again."

"I was. But what I didn't count on was that I could run, but I couldn't hide from my feelings for you."

So she wasn't in this alone. "Why did you come back?" she prompted.

"So many reasons." He laughed, but there was no humor in the sound. "How much time have you got?"

The rest of my life. "Enough. Tell me," she said softly.

"I couldn't leave you." He met her gaze. "I thought I was doing the right thing and it took every ounce of strength to go. But the truth was there all the time if I hadn't been so bullheaded. I could leave, but sooner or later I'd have been back."

"I'm glad it was sooner," she said, shuddering at what could have happened if he hadn't arrived when he did.

"I had a bad feeling and it wouldn't go away. My gut was telling me that Kevin wasn't responsible."

"And you were right. Can you believe that nutcase was going to let his son take the fall for what he did?"

He nodded. "In his twisted way, I'm sure he believes the kid deserved it."

"He told me that," she confirmed.

"The other thing that bothered me was the fire alarm at the restaurant tonight. My gut was telling me it wasn't a fluke and was somehow connected to you. But Kevin is still in custody."

"Your gut is quite the chatterbox." Her mouth curved up, then she turned serious. "Did you call here, a little while after you left?"

He nodded. "I knew you were home, and when you didn't pick up, I got a real bad feeling."

"Is that why you turned off your headlights?"

"You saw that?"

"I thought help was coming." She let out a long breath. "Then it was dark and I thought maybe I had imagined it."

"I'm sorry it gave you a bad few minutes. But if I was right, I wanted surprise on my side."

"So you were on the porch?"

"Yeah. I heard how he blamed you for busting up his family."

"I was trying to distract him. I'm glad I helped Carol and Kevin get away from that man."

"If I'd been too late—" He shook his head. "If he'd hurt you—"

"He didn't. When you rushed in to save my fanny, I was in the process of talking him into submission."

One corner of his mouth quirked up. "You're good, Counselor. If anyone could do it, it's you."

"And is your gut telling you that? Or personal experience?"

"Definitely personal," he said, his eyes darkening.

Hope jump-started her heart. "Oh?"

"I stopped trying because it was easier. Because it didn't hurt. Because I didn't think I could make a difference anymore." He scooped her up in his arms, then, and settled her on his lap. "Tonight I found out you were right and I was wrong. For every one you lose, there's one you can save. And I'm glad that one is you."

She looped her arms around his neck and looked into his eyes. "I need to say something."

"Okay."

"When I wasn't sure whether or not I'd get out of that mess alive, I only had one regret. I'd never told you how I feel about you. I love you, Sam."

"Jamie, I—"

"Let me finish." She rested her forehead against his.

"I love you so much it doesn't even matter if you promise to stay. I'll take whatever you can give."

"What if I give you my heart?" He cupped her cheek in his palm as their gazes locked. "I love you, Jamie. I want to spend the rest of my life with you. I want to have babies with you."

"I'd like that." The words sounded so inadequate to describe the happiness bubbling inside her. And nothing could put a damper on it. "So you'll be wanting your old job back with the LAPD."

He shook his head. "There's a rumor going around that Charity City is a wonderful place to raise a family."

She didn't think it could get bigger or better, but her joy sizzled and sparked and exploded like fireworks on the Fourth of July. "My folks will be over the moon."

"They won't have to worry about you any more. From now on, I'll take care of you. I'll do my best to make you happy."

"I am happy. And your best is all I could ever hope for. *You* are the best."

"Does that mean you'll marry me?" he asked.

"Yes."

He let out a long breath, then settled his mouth on hers, a tender pledge to seal his solemn promise.

She smiled. "Do you remember that first day you showed up in my office?"

"I'll never forget. It was the best day of my life."

"Mine, too. But little did I know when you said something's gotta give that *something* would be me."

"I'll take you," he said, kissing her senseless.

And they would spend the rest of their lives giving and taking, compromising and negotiating. But through it all, they would always be loving each other.

Epilogue

Jamie Brimstone looked around the table—three of them couldn't fit in a booth anymore. She smiled at her friends—Charity Wentworth, Abby Dixon and Molly O'Donnell. Brushing a thumb over the platinum band with inset diamonds on the ring finger of her left hand, she gave thanks for her husband, who was the love of her life, and these very special women, who were all facing big changes in their own lives.

Beautiful, blond Charity looked at each of them and their gently rounding tummies. "Six months pregnant. I feel like it's high school again, the cool kids are having a party and no one invited me."

Redheaded Molly O'Donnell made an unladylike sound of dissent. "Yeah, like you'd have any idea how it feels to not be cool."

"I got a taste of it being the chuck wagon cook for Logan Price's roundup," she said.

"And he's one hunky rancher who rounded up more than steers," Jamie pointed out. "When he bought you at the auction, I bet he had no idea he was getting his future wife."

Charity grinned, as she admired the engagement ring on her finger. "It was a surprise to me, too. But I'm happier than I've ever been."

"Ditto," Molly said. "Des and I just found out we're having a Desdemona." Everyone gasped at the news about the baby's sex.

Charity stared. "Please tell me that name is up for negotiation."

"It comes up as more of a threat when he throws out names like Bambi and Fawn. I just tell him we'll name the baby after him."

Jamie saw her friend's newfound confidence and remembered all her father's manipulation. Carter Richmond's schemes had nearly ruined Molly's chance for happiness. "How are things with your dad?"

"He's finally getting the message that Des and I won't tolerate his interference. I think he's looking forward to being a grandfather and won't risk being cut off from his granddaughter. Tell me Des and I aren't the only spineless parents who decided to find out what we're having."

Abby smiled as she tucked a strand of straight brown hair behind her ear. "Riley and I couldn't stand the suspense. We're having a boy."

"That's wonderful, Ab," Jamie said.

"Riley's pretty excited." She grinned. "He says between Kimmie and the new baby, his kids will keep him pretty busy."

Jamie shifted uncomfortably in her chair. "This little guy is running out of room."

"A boy?" Charity said.

Jamie nodded. "Sam is excited and sweet and protective."

Because of the baby she'd lost. Because he loved her. Because he would never let her down. And because that night six months before—and the memory of how easily their happiness could have been blown away—made them grateful for every day together and every wonderful blessing that came their way.

There was no way to thank her parents for giving Sam to her. But she didn't need to. They heartily approved of the marriage and could hardly wait to spoil their grandson.

Sam was still the only one who knew about the baby she'd lost, and she planned to keep it that way. Because if not for him, this life might never have been.

She would spend every day loving him with all her heart and didn't doubt for a second that he would do the same.

* * * * *

If you enjoyed what you just read,
then we've got an offer you can't resist!

Take 2 bestselling love stories FREE!

Plus get a FREE surprise gift!

SILHOUETTE *Romance*®

COMING NEXT MONTH

#1818 CHASING DREAMS—Cara Colter
Book-smart and reserved, Jessica King instinctively knows she
needs someone to bring her inner wild child out. And though she's
engaged to a somewhat stuffy academic, something tells her that
earthy mechanic Garner Blake, whom she has just met, may be
more the man of her dreams…. But can she find the courage now to
listen to her heart and not her head?

#1819 WISHING AND HOPING—Susan Meier
Word on the street is that Tia Capriotti is suddenly marrying
Drew Wallace, a longtime neighbor *and* her father's best friend. But
inquiring minds want to know—is there something political afoot in
their courtship? And what is that subtle bulge at her belly?

#1820 IF THE SLIPPER FITS—Elizabeth Harbison
Concierge; browbeaten orphan—they might be one and the same,
with the way Prince Conrad's stepmother treats hostess Lily Tilden
in her own boutique hotel. To uncover the jewel that is hers and
Conrad's love, Lily must first overcome the royal tricks of this
woman, who seems to have studied carefully the wicked women
of yore!

#1821 THE PARENT TRAP—Lissa Manley
Divorcée Jill Lindstrom and widower Brandon Clark each just
wanted to leave hectic lives and open landmark restaurants in the
small Oregon town. But their cooking mixtures seem bland when
compared to the elaborate schemes their daughters concoct to give
the pair a taste of how delicious their lives could be together….

SRCNM0506